P9-AZV-745

The White Doe

Most glorious sunset! and a ray
Survives—the twilight of this day—
In that fair Creature whom the fields
Support, and whom the forest shields.

—WORDSWORTH'S
White Doe of Rylstone

RICHARD CHURCH

The White Doe

Illustrated by John Ward R.A.

THE JOHN DAY COMPANY
NEW YORK

*To my grandchildren
and great-grandchildren
in Europe, America, and
New Zealand,
this tale of England,
in 1910*

1 Young Neighbor

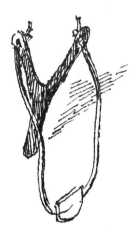

"It will make no difference," said Billy Lander to his friend Tom Winter. "What won't?" replied Tom sulkily. He was sulky because he was miserable, and he was miserable because he didn't want to face the fact that a change was coming into their lives and particularly into their friendship. He knew only too well what Billy meant, but he had to pretend not to understand, because it was about something which he wanted not to happen.

Billy Lander was going away to boarding school.

"I tell you it won't," said Billy. He knew what was

going on in Tom's mind, and it made him almost angry.

"This is a fine thing, and on our birthday too!"

That reminder cheered Tom a little, and he nodded, even smiled weakly as Billy punched him affectionately in the small of the back, nearly toppling him off the five-bar gate on which they sat.

That gate divided the end of a forest ride, or lane, from the open scrub country which led to the cliffs and the sea, a mile away, beyond the rising ground, marked with gorse bushes, juniper and twisted hawthorn trees, which caught the sea winds and held them off from the forest. "Born on the same day," said Tom, still brooding on the past and the change that threatened it.

"Well, we've got on all right, haven't we?" said Billy. "I can't help it if I have to follow in Father's footsteps. You know what he's like. Tradition, and all that!"

"He's all right, your father!"

"Who said he wasn't? But he never forgets that he's the squire of these broad acres!" And Billy spoke bitterly, waving an arm to indicate his future inheritance and to resent the burden of it. "You'll still be here, won't you?" he added.

"Will I?" said Tom. "But I'll only be a woodman, like my dad."

"Who's the snob now?" said Billy angrily. But he instantly relented.

"Look, Tom, we've grown up together, done everything together. You don't need to mope, spoiling the rest of the holiday. There's another month yet."

Tom had no chance to consider this good advice, for almost before it was delivered, Billy's corgi, whose name was Pembroke, suddenly sat up, stamped his forepaws

2

on the ground, like a soldier on sentry duty, and began to growl—that deep internal sound peculiar to the breed.

"What's up, Pembro?" said his master.

But the rumbling continued.

Then, in the distance, a figure moved, stealing from bush to bush, across the line of vision.

"Who is it?" said Tom. "Stranger on our land?"

"It's those new people. They've just moved into the big house beyond the village. Mother calls it the White Elephant because we've never been able to let it. But these people have bought it and have smartened it up. You've not been down there lately, Tom. Rather a hermit, aren't you?"

"I don't like streets," said Tom.

"And you don't like people very much. Do you good to mix a bit."

"I mix with you all right."

Billy ignored this. He was watching for the stranger to reappear from behind a hawthorn tree, where red berries glowed in the hot autumn evening sunlight, which flooded along the open country, and glittered on the sea beyond, making it heavy and metallic.

He frowned as he concentrated. "He's the son. A bit older than us, I'd say. They came to tea to let us know what they intended to do to make the White Elephant fit for them to live in. Father took a poor view of that. So did I, but Mother said everyone to his own taste, and if they can afford five bathrooms for four people, why not?"

"Four people?"

"There's a daughter. She's older than the boy—and a different mother."

"Her mother dead, then?"

3

"I wouldn't know, but the boy's mother is pretty smart. Takes a lot of upkeep, I bet!"

"Just rich, then?"

"Rolling in it, and proud of it."

"The boy, too?"

"Dry up; he's making toward us. Let's be civil."

As the figure drew near, after emerging from the shelter of the hawthorn, he was seen to be rather plump, but agile. He carried a large slingshot—a commercial one, made of metal, a deadly-looking object.

"Hello," he said, addressing himself to Billy and ignoring both Tom Winter and Pembroke the corgi, though the latter was rumbling ominously and rolling his eyes as though waiting for the word of attack from his master. His hindquarters had risen from the ground, but otherwise he had not moved. He was well trained. Billy Lander, like his father, had a way with dogs.

"You on the hunt?" asked the stranger, flourishing his slingshot.

"No, just sitting on a gate," said Billy. "And this is Tom Winter."

"Sitting on the gate, too," said the hunter, still without looking at Tom. "Good open country," he added. "I bagged a thrush, but it limped away into the wood, not worth following up."

"Oh," said Tom, as though stung by a wasp.

"This is Harold Sims," said Billy quickly, fearing trouble. He knew Tom was funny about birds and beasts —almost one of them in his shy ways and his quick instincts.

"Tom Winter?" said Harold Sims. "I haven't heard of you. Where do you fit in?"

"My father is woodman here," said Tom, very quietly.

4

Sims looked puzzled. He stared first at Billy and then at Tom. "Oh, I see," he said. But he didn't see, and a long silence followed, one of those silences during which time stands still and the whole universe becomes a looker-on.

The spell was broken by an outburst of forlorn, solitary song from a robin, who had flickered from nowhere into the yellowing foliage of a maple that overhung the gate. His red breast could be seen, conspicuously rusty amid the hectic leaves.

Harold Sims became possessed. His eyes glittered, his mouth widened into a grin that showed his teeth. Steadily he took aim.

In an instant, Tom was off the gate. He leaped forward and struck down the raised arm. "You don't do that!" he cried, and this set Pembroke to barking. The robin disappeared as mysteriously as it had come.

"What d'you mean?" said Sims, furious. "You lout! You spoiled my shot!"

"He's no lout," said Billy quietly, approaching slowly from the gate and stepping in front of Tom, who was lost between rage and confusion. "Tom's my friend, you see. And we don't go in for casual slaughter in this part of the country."

Sims glared fiercely; then he relaxed, and a sneer took the place of the rage which had made him such an ugly customer. But the second mood was even more ugly. "Oh, a bird sanctuary, is it? I've heard of them."

He turned, and shambled off, making westward as he murmured something about cranks and what his father would have to say about yokels and interfering busybodies.

Billy looked at Tom, after they had watched the figure

5

disappear round an outpost of the woodland. "You've trodden on a wasps' nest, Tom."

But Tom was still speechless. His face had paled, and one of his hands was trembling. "Wounding a thrush!" he said at last.

"But you saved the redbreast," retorted Billy. "Let's get away from here. Somehow it smells."

As they retreated along the woodland ride after closing the gate, Billy added, "You'll have to watch him, Tom. He looks to me to have a long memory."

Twilight began to gather in the wood, though the sunshine still gilded the tops of the taller trees here and there, a pine, a spindly oak hemmed in by its neighbors, a beech that had made its own clearing round its wide-spread branches.

As the boys turned into the cross ride that led to the cottage, Tom's home, on the road that ran through the forest from the village to end at the sea abruptly where the cliff had fallen away, they heard a distant trumpeting deeper in the wood.

"There it is!" whispered Tom. "It's the fallow. The bucks are fierce at this time of the year. Listen! The mating cry!"

They stood, awe-stricken. The sound came muffled through the trees, broken and brittle, but it filled the air with a challenge, fierce and unbiddable. Nothing could gainsay that savage music.

The boys looked at each other almost guiltily, as though nature were shaming them.

"I bet Father is listening," said Billy. "He'll be thinking of the herd, his precious herd."

Then he looked sideways at his unaccountable companion, a gleam of mischief in his friendly eye. "Different proposition from picking off songbirds with a slingshot!"

Tom accepted that without a word, and they walked on together as darkness drew down its curtain over the forest. Pembroke had gone on in front.

2 Tom's Father

This story about Tom Winter belongs to the
early years of the twentieth century. People in England
at that time kept to what was called their "station in
life", but as can be seen from Tom's friendship with
Billy Lander, this did not prevent close relationships
between master and servant. Often they served each
other, and wages had little to do with it.

So it need not seem strange that when Tom lifted the
latch of the cottage door and entered the living room, he
saw his mother through a haze of golden light, from the
oil lamp on the table laid for late tea. The tablecloth
reflected the light from the white frosted-glass shade and
made a homely picture of Mrs. Winter, who sat at the
table darning socks, with her workbasket beside. It over-
flowed with wools, cottons, bits and pieces of material,
needlecase, and scissors.

"You're late, Tom," she said. "Been out with Master
William, I expect. Inseparable, you two. What's to come
of it, I don't know. Gives you ideas, that's what it
does."

Tom said nothing. He had heard all this before. His
mother was not one to presume, as she said. She knew her
place, was another of her sober sayings. That was why she

always called Billy "Master William", intending this as a
lesson for Tom.

When she and her husband entered Sir George
Lander's service the year before Tom and Billy were
born, they came from an estate whose owner was one of
the old school and treated his tenants and workmen
accordingly. The home there had been little more than a
mud hut, and Tom's father had made his own window
for it. The couple brought that window with them, when
they came to the woodman's cottage at the edge of the
forest, for they expected similar conditions to those they
had left. But they found an ample casement with leaded
lights, and the window made by Tom's father was put
into the workshop behind the cottage, also built by Tom's
father from timber provided by the Squire.

Life was very different under this genial, but strict,

master. He paid small wages, but he gave in kind: kindling, logs, coal at Christmas, and often something for the table when a pig or a bullock was killed, sometimes a joint of venison when the herd was being thinned.

Even though Sir George was harsh toward poachers, especially if they were outsiders and townsfolk, he said nothing about the occasional rabbit or pair of pigeons that entered the pot over the kitchen range in the Winters' cottage. But he was very protective of the game creatures: the grouse, the pheasants, the partridges, the hares. About his deer he was fanatical. Perhaps the friendship between his heir and the woodman's boy was acceptable to him because he had noticed Tom's love of animals and the boy's uncanny knowledge of their ways.

"Father's late too," said Mrs. Winter, with a sigh, while she tidied up the workbasket and stuffed the pile of socks under the lid. "Better see about the supper. Expect you're ready for it. Just like menfolk, always homing at mealtime."

To prove her words, Tom's father entered, from the back kitchen. He had been around to leave his tools in the shed.

"Smells good, eh, Tom?" he said.

"Something special tonight, isn't it, Mother?"

"You don't need to advertise it," said Mrs. Winter, and as she lifted the lid of the pot simmering on the stove built into the huge chimney place, a delectable whiff of something richer than rabbit suffused the living room. "A proper beauty, he was," said Arthur Winter. "Good job you weren't about, Tom. I flung a wedge and caught him amidships as he lolloped across the clearing. 'Tisn't often a hare makes so bold."

10

His wife looked uneasily around. "You needn't say what 'tis, man."

Father and son went out to the kitchen to wash. Mrs. Winter ran her little household with great discipline, for she had been trained in domestic service before she married. She liked things to be just so and her family to be nice in their domestic habits.

So they sat decorously at table, with a spotlessly white cloth, their faces bright in the lamplight reflected from it. Most of the furniture was homemade, Arthur Winter's rustic handiwork, but it was so highly polished under his wife's daily rubbings that it shone even brighter than the three happy faces, into which the jugged hare, with homegrown potatoes and a full-blown cauliflower, was discreetly disappearing.

"I reckon I shall be stiff as a post in the morning," said Arthur. "Been on at it all day felling that great beech which stood at the crossways by Sunset Bridge westward. 'Tis a pity to bring him down, and they up at the Hall will see the gap, I reckon. But Squire wanted him down, he said, for the timber to make a tallboy after it has weathered a year or two. He's set on beechwood furniture. If you've ever been up at the Hall, you can see it in plenty."

"I have been," said Tom.

"No," cried his mother incredulously. "That you haven't, surely. Intruding in the Hall?"

"I've been up to Billy's room, often enough. He's got another little room beside it, where he keeps all his tackle and things."

Mrs. Winter was so shocked that she picked up the earthenware pot of jugged hare and carried it out to the scullery, to return with a large bowl of junket, as though to demonstrate her disapproval of her son's boldness in venturing inside the great Hall.

"That don't signify," said Arthur. "Born on the same day, weren't they? You can't go against nature, my dear. I reckon Tom don't presume. He knows his station, like you and me. And we're friendly enough with them at the Hall, aren't we?"

" 'Tisn't the same," she said obstinately, and left it at that, while her husband told them of the felling of the tree and how the gamekeeper, Peter Apps, and the estate carpenter, Jeremy Hogg (who was later to use the timber to make the tallboy for a guest's bedroom), helped him with the roping, the lopping of the branches and the later stage of sawing and chopping through the base of the bole.

"Can't think why the Squire is so set on beech for his furniture, when there is plenty of ripe oak in the forest. All right for chairs, I reckon, but an oak cupboard will outlast any beechwood, pretty though it be in color."

They discussed this over the junket, and then Arthur added further to his account of the day's heavy work.

"That much less food for the deer, too. They loved gathering under that old fellow and feeding on the beechmast. 'Twas ankle-deep under him. That's what drew them there—and a pretty sight they made around his silvery trunk, with the sunlight dappling their coats. Pride of the forest, they are."

"Did you hear the bucks trumpeting, Dad?" asked Tom, as though to remind him of another aspect of the herd's characteristics.

His father ignored that and went on, "Those roots will never come out, I'll lay. They spread underground as wide as the branches overhead. And some of those lower

12

branches were as thick as my waist. How we did sweat with that double-handed saw. Peter said he was handier with his gun than with that tool. I reckon he is, too. But he had a dig at me: said it wouldn't do for me to come and help him with his job. Friendly-like, but he was getting at something. Wonder if he knows about that stewpot? But there's no ill-will in Peter. It's trust and trust again with him: but a wink on the sly!"

"You're talking too much, Mr. Winter," said his wife. "And you still haven't put that new leg in my washing stool, which I shall want for Monday."

"I'll do it now, Mother," he said, and he took down a storm lantern from a hook in the scullery ceiling, lit it, and opened the door into the yard.

Mrs. Winter took advantage of this to throw out the hare bones from the plates, and these were followed by Caesar, the tomcat, who had been cadging in vain during the meal.

Father and son disappeared into the night, and the dim light from the lantern flickered up and down the features of the yard between the cottage and the shed, bringing to ghostly life the green stuff in the vegetable patch, the bare soil where the potatoes had been lifted, the fruit bushes and an old, laden apple tree. The yellow light thinned away into darkness toward the forest.

"There it is, Dad," whispered Tom, unlatching the door of the shed.

From the forest there came the bell-like trumpeting, fierce, yet frightened, as though the deer were bewildered by the instincts driving them to this seasonal madness.

3   A Parting

Four weeks later the day dawned which was to be the last before Billy Lander went away to boarding school. He came to the cottage early that evening, so early that Tom had only just got home from the village school.

Mrs. Winter looked surprised and a little anxious when he appeared, but Tom took the visit quite calmly, though he said nothing. He knew Billy had come to say good-bye, and he was feeling miserable.

They had lived like brothers; more friendly than brothers, because the difference in their homelife and parentage caused them to be sensitive of each other's feelings. They were oddly polite, one to the other, as though to show the world—well, just to show the world!

The four weeks had been full of adventure, though the last one was restricted to evening outings, because Tom had started school; the holidays ending as soon as harvesting was over.

Mrs. Winter gave each of the boys a slice of cake, and off they went together, eating it as they opened the the gate behind the work-shed, which led to a footpath trodden by Arthur Winter alone, a private entry into the forest. The trees dwarfed the figures of the boys, which

quickly merged into the shadowy interior of the woodland way. They walked single file through the hundred
yards or so, their boots brushed by the tangle of brier,
dog's mercury, bracken already changing color, and the
variety of dried-out grasses and herbs of the departed
summer.

By the time they reached a wider ride and turned along
it, the cake was consumed, and they could walk side by
side. But they were curiously shy, knowing that this was
the moment of something coming to an end.

"Mother had those people from the White Elephant to
tea yesterday," said Billy, decapitating a man-high
thistle with an oak plant which he had brought with him

15

from the store in that little spare room described by Tom to his mother. "The brave hunter was there, as well as the stepsister. She's quite different: older, and it's obvious there's no love lost between them. But she keeps calm, and that's not easy, I'd say, with that character around. He plumped himself down in an armchair before either his mother or the girl were seated. Father picked a cushion from the couch and put it behind the little bounder's back. 'Make yourself comfortable,' he said. I nearly smothered myself, trying not to laugh. Then Father walked out and left us to it. I'd have gone too; but Mother gave me a look, and I had to stay."

"What's the father like?"

"He didn't come, though they all had accepted Mother's invitation. Perhaps that's why Father left the party, but I think he couldn't stand Master Harold's manners."

Tom was not much interested. His attention was given to the society of the forest, its perpetual business amid the seeming silence and solitude, though things were quiet enough on this autumn evening. There was no bird music, though a distant cry from an owl sounded a warning that winter was on its way.

The air was quite still, and not a leaf moved. Yet from time to time one and then another detached themselves from their twigs and fluttered down—a tiny, dry process. But that too was prophetic, slightly ominous. The path was already littered with such forebodings.

The boys stopped to examine a cluster of crimson toadstools. Their curiosity aroused that of a robin, who flew down fearlessly, after uttering a lonely little roulade from his perch above their heads. He stood, knock-kneed, with his red waistcoat thrust out defiantly, and the con-

16

trast of his soft coloring, subdued and feathery, with the enameled brilliance of the domed fungi, filled Tom with delight. "See that?" he whispered, everything else forgotten. "Look, Billy, look!"

Billy was looking, but still being concerned with social matters, he was reminded by the robin's appearance of what happened when Tom attacked Harold Sims. "I wonder if it's the same robin," he said.

Tom was puzzled. He had forgotten the incident. He lived intensely in the present moment, especially out-of-doors. And Harold Sims had not crossed his path since that day.

"When I'm not here, you'd better keep a lookout for him," said Billy. "He was on to me yesterday about you. He's like the elephant. He's got a long memory, and he's still smarting over what he calls your infernal cheek. Oh, yes, you're a low-class cad, Tom Winter!"

He looked at Tom affectionately. Both boys were in an emotional state, and had no means of expressing their feelings.

"Let's get on," said Tom, "and find the big beech tree which Dad has brought down. I don't think he's cut it up yet."

"A rotten shame; I hate the idea," said Billy. "I grumbled to my father, but he said the timber was at its best at this age, and he wants it for Mr. Hogg to work on as soon as it's seasoned. But that'll be a couple of years. Where shall we be then? Sounds like eternity."

"We shan't know each other by that time," said Tom as he walked on.

"Don't talk rot, young Winter," said the cool and worldly-wise Billy Lander. "You take life too hard. You need to grow another skin, to protect yourself."

17

Tom was too simple to understand this. He said nothing; but Billy's good-nature penetrated the gloom, and Tom's attention returned to the things he knew and could understand, the life of the forest and the fields, the cliffs and the sea. This was his own kingdom, and it served him well. "I'm as old as you are," was all he said.

The woodland ride led westward toward the end of the forest that gave on to the home park and the Hall—Billy's home, into which Tom was welcomed far more often than his mother realized.

The boys came upon the beech tree some hundred yards in from the open fields that separated the park from the forest. It still looked majestic, though it stretched supine in the clearing. Some of the upper, smaller branches, which had been left uncut, had struck the ground and penetrated the humuslike soil. But they kept the summit of the tree at an angle, and the whole corpse lay like the skeleton of a mastodon resting on its foreribs. The foliage, still dull green, hung lifeless, and tangled in it drooped the shattered nest of a squirrel.

Perhaps this was the home of the gray squirrel which sat on the fallen trunk, chattering over a beechnut which he held in his paws. He was so intent on his meal that for a while he ignored the human intruders. They watched him turning the nut over and over. The little teeth flashed, and the tail lay along the tree trunk, shuddering with nervous energy, and coiling up and out again as though beating time to the rhythm of the eager jaws at work on the nut.

Then the little fellow saw the boys. His business stopped. He eyed them from those two protruding orbs and in a flash was gone, back into the protection of the upper branches still left on the trunk and from there into a pine

18

from which the fall of the beech had stripped several great fronds and left a gaping wound. But the squirrel was already around the other side of the pine and no doubt at the top of it.

Tom and Billy sat down on the tree trunk, and Tom began to count the rings in the cross-section of the wood, each representing a year of growth. But he had not gone beyond forty when Billy interrupted this rustic arithmetic. "I suppose you won't come up to the Hall while I'm away?"

Tom stopped counting and turned to stroking the smooth bark of the beech. He shook his head sadly. "No occasion to," he said.

"I think my people will expect to see you. They like your visits more than your mother likes mine."

"That's not fair," said Tom. "I can't explain. She thinks I'm intruding; as good as says so."

"Oh, is that it? I don't understand, either. Funny ideas, these grown-ups have. They all seem suspicious of each other. I suppose there's a reason for it. There are some funny people about, and they start young. Here's one such coming. Do we still have to be civil?"

He was right. Harold Sims, without the slingshot, was approaching along the ride recently trodden by Tom and Billy. They waited in silence until he reached them. "I heard you were off to school tomorrow," he said. "I've got two more days yet, so I went to the Hall to find you and was told you were down at the woodman's cottage, and I followed on."

He sounded friendly, but he looked sheepish. The boys responded, however, though Tom had nothing to say.

"What have you got there?" asked Billy.

"Oh, I'm studying anatomy. I picked up these bones

19

in the cottage garden. The woman told me to go out by the back gate as I wanted to find you both."

He put the handful of bones into a game bag slung from his shoulder, and no more was said about the matter. He lingered for a while and was friendly enough, even to Tom, the woodman's son, including him in the conversation as though to persuade him that there was no ill-will over the incident during that first meeting four weeks earlier.

But Tom and Billy were relieved when he left them, for they showed no inclination to move, and he grew bored with nothing to do or what he believed was nothing to do.

"Well, good luck," he said to Billy. "Don't envy you your first term. It's something like hell on earth."

"Depends what you make of it," said Billy Lander, "but thanks for the warning."

After he was lost around the bend of the woodland ride, the two boys were silent and uneasy.

"What's he mean by that?" demanded Tom at last.

"Oh, just the nature of the beast," said Billy. "What did he think I'm expecting, the Garden of Eden?"

"No, I don't mean that about the school. What's all that about studying anatomy?"

Billy was puzzled, and did not reply.

"Those bones he picked up weren't a rabbit's," said Tom.

Before Billy could comment on this half-confession, their gloominess was dispelled by something near at hand.

Tom saw it first. He touched Billy on the sleeve and pointed ahead. A fine fallow buck trotted across the ride, further in the wood where the boys had turned at the junction. It moved so proudly that its hooves gave the impression of stamping audibly on the turf. Its head and neck were carried with equal pride.

It was followed closely by a doe, smaller and even more dainty and paler in color. The westering sun, exploring the opening in the trees along the ride, fell on both creatures as they broke through the path of light, touching the dappled coats with magic.

Some moments later a dozen or more deer followed, but uncertainly, pausing, looking around in confusion, backing, and then moving on again, expectant of being repulsed. Once again the trumpeting rang through the forest, the miniature roar of the mating cry, disappearing among the trees.

"That's a good way out," said Billy. "We'll remember that, Tom, while I'm away. And I'll be home for Christmas. Don't forget that. So good-bye for now."

He left Tom standing by the tree trunk and did not look round until he reached the bend in the ride. Tom had not turned either. He had stood during those few moments with his back to the departing friend, pretending to be concerned only with the herd of deer. But as Billy stopped and looked back, so did Tom. There came from Billy a neat imitation of the trumpeting of the buck. His two hands were spread palm outward above his ears, to represent antlers. Then he was gone.

Tom walked slowly back to the cottage, his footfall as silent on the turf as the forest was silent. Not even the robin's plaintive little song could be heard. He stopped once or twice, to hear his own blood pounding in his veins and to control the lump in his throat. But even in those moments of depression, his eyes were alert, watching the nothingness going on in the woodland, the halted traffic of nature.

4 *Alone*

Tom Winter found life very strange. For the first time since he had begun to move around in the world, he had to move alone, and a forest world is a very big one. An acre of thick woodland is more vast than thirty acres of open country.

Tom was an only child. He lived in a cottage on the fringe of the forest, remote from the village. He attended the village school but made no friends there. He came and went, and that took up the time he might have used out of school hours to play with the boys from the village.

He shared everything with Billy Lander. They both knew the forest and its life. Now Tom was left alone there. He still had to follow its command. It was still his master. Indeed, without Billy to take part in this powerful relationship, Tom felt even more compelled by the mystery of the forest—its ever-changing character, the myriad moods and voices, its lights and shadows, its elusiveness.

The autumn passed into winter, and Tom's walk to and from school was shadowed by twilight.

One November afternoon he was tempted by a clear sunset to make a detour, intending to reach home not by the lane, but through one of the woodland rides. He knew that labyrinth by heart. He had even drawn his own map of it—not a very accurate and scientific one, like the six-inch survey maps, but serviceable to his purpose of knowing his way in every part of those hundreds of acres, their streams, dells, rises, and the disused quarry long since overgrown with a plantation of sycamores, a brighter green patch rarely seen by human eye. Sycamores have a habit of spreading their family around them. Nobody penetrated there, except Peter Apps, the gamekeeper, and Tom Winter.

Tom made his way there that afternoon, knowing that darkness was falling. But the trees were bare, and a thin flurry of snow made a bright pattern on the paths through the wood. The cold was intense, and frost filled the air and sky with heaviness. Everything was brittle, and Tom's boots crunched on the twigs and fallen leaves as though he were walking on sugar.

He was humming to himself. The frosty nightfall and the deep silence were a challenge. He was in his own world here and had no fear of its moods.

Then, as he approached the dip of the quarry, he heard other footsteps. He stood below, and looking up to the bare sycamores rooted perilously at the top edge of the pit, he saw old Peter Apps, a bulky figure with a sack around his shoulders, a bag on his back, and a gun sloping barrel downward under his arm.

"That you, young Tom?" said the old man. His kindly voice sounded like a shout in the still air. It echoed from the trees behind Tom, who stood in the little clearing of shale and tumbled stone in the bed of the quarry.

" 'Tis late to be out as far as this, boy. What's taken you to venture so far?"

23

"I'm on my way from school, Mr. Apps," said Tom. "I like to come home through the trees."

The old man chuckled. "Ha! like your dad. We'll make a woodman of you yet. 'Tis a skillful trade too, and regular. No danger of being out of a place for a good tree master, such as your dad. You follow him that way, Tom."

The frost seemed to rattle on his words and to carry them down to the boy staring upward into the dusk. The bare branches were still silhouetted against the southwestern sky, where the sunset lingered. But the gamekeeper beneath them was almost invisible. Tom saw the vague figure move.

"Lay by a moment, lad. I'll keep you company and beg a cup o' tea from your mother. I've got a message to leave from Squire, who's just got back from his travels abroad. Wants to see your dad about something particular. Can't think why; that beech is down, and there's nothing to be done to it for a long while."

This eloquent speech was delivered as he made his way down the rock-stepped path to the bottom of the quarry. He eased the bag off his back and handed it to the boy. "Here! Your bones are younger than mine. You carry the bag, and we'll have a look inside it when we get to your mother's kitchen table."

They plodded on, the boy in front and the old gamekeeper chatting away behind him. Peter Apps spent so much of his life wandering about alone over the huge estate that on his occasional encounters with a human being he unloaded his pent-up thoughts through an endless monologue.

Tom only half-heard. His attention was mainly given, as usual, to the goings-on of nature—bird and beast, and

24

all the still things, the plant life and the secrets of the soil. Though nothing was happening in the near darkness of the winter nightfall, Tom knew by instinct that the silence, the deadness, hid a multitude of activities, the hidden preparations for another year.

That alertness made him think of Billy Lander, with whom he had always shared this sixth sense—the lore of the forest, and indeed of open country, too, as well as the sea not far away.

But Peter Apps was still talking, and Tom suddenly focused his attention on what the old man was telling him. "That young lad newly come here. You know him, Tom? Proper mischievous he be, I reckon. They've been at the big house a few months now, and here he is walking around with a gun and a dog—unbiddable animal, too. I warned him one day when the brute coursed a hare and drove it across my way."

Tom stopped and turned to Peter Apps. "What's that?" he said, "that boy's got a gun? He had a slingshot when Billy and I met him, and he'd just wounded a thrush and let it escape."

"That so?" said Peter Apps. "That's not right, Tom. I reckon he comes from town, and don't know our country ways."

Then his thoughtful mood changed, and he prodded Tom in the back as they resumed their way to the cottage. "That young rascal ain't the only one to fancy a hare."

Tom heard this only distantly, as something vaguely threatening; a distant mutter of thunder. He could not allow himself to think about it, but at the back of his mind he knew what the old man meant.

Evidently there was no ill intention in Peter's remark, for when he entered the kitchen by the back door from the garden which Arthur Winter kept so trim, he took the heavy bag from Tom's shoulder, even before he greeted Mrs. Winter, who was busy at her ironingboard in the living room. She came into the kitchen as Peter opened the bag and took out three wood pigeons, rather lean, but lovely in their gray-blue plumage. "A good bag today, Mary. You can do with a pigeon for your men, I reckon?"

"That be very kind of you, Mr. Apps. They've got healthy appetites that keep me busy, I must say."

She felt the birds, taking them up one by one. Tom stared moodily at his mother's hands as they explored the dead birds. He saw the plumage already bedraggled and the eyes lusterless. He could say nothing, but a kind of numbness gripped him. He felt ashamed of something, he did not know what.

"Squire's back," said Peter Apps, "and he told me to say he'd be down in the wood on Saturday morning to have a look at that beech tree which Arthur felled; back in September, wasn't it? Wants to talk to Arthur about it. That puzzles me. Can't think what there is to say about it at this stage."

"Ah, well, he's got something in mind," said Mrs. Winter easily. "There'll be some planting up to talk about, daresay."

"Maybe so," said Peter Apps, picking up his gun and slinging the lightened bag on his back. "Proper dark now," he said, as he left by the front door, with Mrs. Winter seeing him out. "Arthur not back yet, neither. Up to no mischief, I hope, Mary."

She could not see the twinkle in his eye as he said this, for he was looking outward into the darkness, but she must have known what he meant, and she spoke sharply, on the defensive. "There's no mischief in my man, Mr. Apps."

"Ah, well," he said, "stick up for your own. That's woman's way."

Even though she heard him chuckling as he strode down to the front gate, she shut the door frowning with anxiety.

5 A Warning

Next Saturday morning Arthur Winter took Tom with him. He knew that his son was popular up at the Hall. For himself, he saw the Squire so seldom that he was shy whenever he met him. Most of his dealings with authority were through the estate carpenter, Jeremy Hogg, not so friendly a character as Peter Apps. Hogg was proud of his craft as carpenter and joiner.

The weather had changed, and the forest was enveloped in mist, a warm wet mist that soaked into the trees and brought out the winter colors, seeming to light them up from within. The fallen leaves that carpeted the rides gleamed like bronze medals. Every twig had a drop of water hanging, and as the drops fell, the whole forest murmured with the pattering.

"Proper old day," said Arthur, who walked ahead carrying a long-handled ax and several coils of rope. Tom was burdened with a two-handled saw wrapped in sacking and a treacle can full of grease.

"There's a half-dozen oaks Mr. Hogg has flared," said Arthur. "We might as well take one of them down after Squire has had a look around. 'Tisn't often he comes out like this. Usually leaves it to Mr. Hogg, who won't like interference. He's proper touchy when Squire speaks direct to any of us on the estate."

He might have been talking to himself, for Tom was not listening. He had just seen an owl sitting in the middle of the ride, hunched up, with its eyes hooded. As the humans approached, its eyelids blinked open, and the bright orbs glared out. But like Tom, it was not interested, and it made no movement as father and son walked past, their footfalls silent on the carpet of dead leaves, but not silent enough to reassure a spider whose web draped, lacy with mist, like a silk handkerchief between the bare boughs overhanging the path. The spider scuttled up to hide under the branch and in so doing attracted Tom's attention. The boy stopped and would have explored this tiny drama, had he not been so laden and at the bidding of his father, who was impatient and did not pause.

"Come on, boy," he said, "out of sight is out of mind in this fog."

"I'd not be lost here, Dad," said Tom proudly. "I know my way blindfold."

"Don't you be so high-minded. Somebody will surely put you down else." Arthur laughed as he added, "You learn from your mother. She's humble enough, a bit more so than need be sometimes. Frightened of her own shadow, she is, when it comes to social occasions. Comes of living so isolated, I suppose. But it can't be helped. A good situation goes with it, Tom. Mark you that. And you will take my place when my day is done."

Arthur's admonitions to his son, however, were always delivered with an air of sly humor, as though there were a conspiracy between man and boy. So Tom did not take them too seriously. He heeded more, and learned more, from his father's kindliness than from what he said.

Suddenly out of the mist there came a disturbance, and

Tom was as instant in his response to it. The fallow buck
loomed up, trotted swiftly across the junction of the four
rides, and melted again into the mist, which swirled about
after this disturbance, almost disguising the doe, with the
mottled gray coat, who followed close behind the buck

and was as quickly lost. There was no sign of the rest of the herd. "Bless me," said Arthur. "They've been disturbed, and not by us. Reckon that pair is mating."

Voices sounded in the mist, and a moment later the woodman and his son recognized Sir George Lander, followed by Jeremy Hogg. "Ah, there you are, Winter," said the Squire. "We've lost our way in this fog. Thought I knew my own woodland like the back of my hand. Good morning then—and you, Tom. Bit of a lone wolf, aren't you, without Billy to aid and abet? Less mischief, I've no doubt. It's when dogs hunt in couples that they think up trouble. There, don't look so solemn, boy. We must all take a bit of jockeying, eh, Hogg?"

But Hogg disapproved of this overfriendliness between master and man. He ignored the Squire's jocularity and spoke bluntly to the woodman. "You getting those oaks down, Winter? No? Well, better get on with the job. But we'll have a look at this beech you felled awhile back. I want unflawed planks; is it free of canker?"

"Aye, Mr. Hogg," said Arthur, respectfully but still with that glint of mischievous humor in his voice. It was this that made Sir George interested in him, and through him in Tom Winter. Maybe the close friendship between Tom and the Squire's son would not have been allowed had not that interest existed.

Arthur Winter added, "We're not far from the beech. It's passed you in the fog, if you be come from the Hall. It stood almost on the edge of the wood, tall enough to be missed when you look from the windows on the forest side."

He led the way, a hundred yards or less, to the beech. Its foliage still clung, but frost had turned the leaves to a rich umber, the color of a golden retriever's coat. A

32

rabbit scuttled away and disappeared down a moss-framed burrow, which had escaped the human activity when the tree was felled. The flat table of the stump, so cleanly cut, shone like raw flesh in the damp air.

"My word, that's a beauty," said Sir George. "Pity we stripped that pine, Winter."

He missed nothing.

"Yes, sir. But we had a fair wind come that day, though we had him nicely roped. Pretty close it was, too—not much clearance."

"I suppose not. Well, I don't like mutilated trees. Hadn't we better bring that pine down, too, when we are clearing other conifers?"

Jeremy Hogg broke in. He did not like matters of policy being taken out of his hands. "I had that in mind, Sir George. But we must get these oaks down first, for the wood will take a long time to season. Valuable stuff, too."

"Quite, quite," said Sir George, fully aware of Mr. Hogg's self-importance, but willing to use it. He was, however, too fond of Arthur Winter to bring it into play in his next approach to his woodman. He moved away from the tree, which Hogg was examining more closely with an expert eye.

"Winter!" said the Squire, drawing Arthur aside and speaking more quietly than was his habit, "I want a word with you. I've just had evidence brought me that the bones of hare have been found in your garden. You know what I feel about poaching game, especially when strangers break in. I'll ask you to be more careful in future and not to flaunt the evidence. It might lead to trouble. I speak as a magistrate, Winter, and that's something I don't expect to do with one of my own people."

Arthur Winter flushed. "That fair puzzles me, sir," he said. "I ain't that kind of a fool, after all. Looks like a bit of interfering to me."

Sir George looked at him, and a gleam of sympathy displaced the official disapproval in his eyes. "Maybe! Maybe!" he said. "Well, that's enough. But I don't like trouble on the estate, and poaching is poaching, Arthur."

They said no more and returned to Jeremy Hogg and Tom, the latter absorbed in the technical observations of the expert worker in wood, whose mastery of his craft perhaps justified his professional snobbery.

After some further discussion on woodland matters, the Squire and estate carpenter left and were quickly swallowed up in the fog, long before they reached the bend in the ride around which Tom and Billy had watched Harold Sims disappear. Tom remembered that autumn day and the scene of his parting from Billy.

"Won't do, mooning about here, boy," said Arthur briskly. "Might as well get something done, though this half-darkness don't encourage us. Wake yourself up, Tom! You're dreaming, lad!"

He was too animated, and Tom looked at his face, flushed with more than weather. The father saw the look of inquiry.

"That fair puzzles me, Tom," he said. "How did Squire get to know about that hare I knocked over? Why, 'twas weeks ago!"

"I know, Dad," said Tom doggedly.

"You know! How do you know?"

Tom told him, as they trudged through the dripping woods, of the incident on that unforgettable day when he last saw Billy Lander; the interruption of those miserable moments by Harold Sims, carrying the ribcase of the

34

hare in his hand, and smoothly slipping it into his bag as he said that he was studying anatomy. U, S, 1481997

"Why, we've done him no harm, surely? What the mischief was he up to, telling on us like that? I don't understand such ways. 'Tisn't honest!"

Then Tom confessed about the first meeting with the newcomer and how the life of a singing robin had been saved at the expense of what Billy had called "being civil."

The perplexity cleared from Arthur Winter's face, but he shook his head after some moments of slow cogitation.

"That be a bad business, Tom. But it wasn't your fault, lad, though I don't go with the idea of playing rough with anybody. It don't make life easy, I tell you."

"That's what Billy said," Tom answered ruefully. "He warned me to watch out, and now we know."

"Aye, now we know. But now we'll forget it, Tom. Doesn't do to brood. You see how the Squire took it. He might have been proper nasty, and Mr. Hogg looking on, mind you. The thought of it fair turned me over, Tom. Better not say a word to your mother, or I'll never dare bring in a hare again!"

He had recovered confidence in himself, and the thought of his careful wife's being the cause of the betrayal made him laugh aloud. "Proper young fox, that boy," he said, throwing down the burden at the foot of an oak tree marked with a flare of white paint.

Father and son worked together through the rest of the morning. Tom shinned up the tree and tied two guide ropes, which his father spread almost at right angles and pegged into the ground. After sawing through some lower branches and dragging them aside, he set Tom at the other end of the two-handled saw, first chipping a hold for its teeth in the bole about a foot from the ground. Acorns crunched under their boots as they took their footing on opposite sides of the trunk.

It was slow work, for the tree was a veteran, with a base as large as a table. Flakes of bark, green as rusty copper with moss and flecked with tiny fungi, flew from the gleaming teeth of the saw. From time to time Arthur spread a fistful of grease along the blade, yellowing the steel. Then at it again they went, biting into the harder, inner rings of the timber, drawing sawdust out of the gash at every pull to and fro, to and fro. The moan of the metal

36

rang like music through the forest, a monotonous note that dulled the ears of the two at work.

But it did not prevent them from hearing the distant sound of the church clock striking twelve, a faint announcement through the trees, and the November silences, lonely and sad.

"Another five minutes, Tom, and we're through," said Arthur, stretching to ease his back. He wiped the sweat from his face with one hand, while examining the palm of the other. "Got any blisters?" he asked, with a happy grin. The warning from Sir George was quite forgotten.

Arthur's calculation was right. After some five minutes of further labor, the great tree trembled and stood seemingly a little more upright, as though striving against its fate. Three more double strokes, and there came a moaning sound, followed by a lurch. Another pause, a recoil, and slowly the oak keeled over and crashed to the ground, hitting it with a thump that reverberated through the bodies of the two executioners.

"That be it," said Arthur, moving without further delay to unfasten the ropes and re-coil them.

The job had been carried out so neatly that no damage was done to neighboring trees. Another oak nearby was flashed with white paint. With the two of them down, the break in the forest would be considerably widened. A little silver birch stood isolated, lanky and trembling under its exposure. A pungent smell rose from the wounds of the oak—a leathery smell of tannin.

All was still again, as man and boy gathered up their tools and walked away, single file, into the mist and out of sight. In a few moments even the sound of their movement ceased, and there was nothing except the drip, drip of the mist through the winter branches.

37

6 Tom Makes Another Friendship

As the winter days passed, Tom brooded over the spiteful trick played by Harold Sims. Nothing seemingly came out of it, thanks to Sir George's good nature and his liking for the Winter family. Indeed, Tom might also have thanked young Sims, because the incident had brought father and son even closer together. It made Tom feel older and protective of his easy-going father. There was a touch of his mother in him, too, and this made him anxious about Sims. Was this stranger likely to be satisfied, or was he watching for another opportunity to injure Tom, who had upset his vanity? So Tom asked himself, again and again, though he had no cause to, for the days passed, and Sims, too, was away at school.

Christmas approaching, and soon Billy Lander would be home again. But so would Harold Sims. This realization gave Tom an uneasy feeling, but one morning, a week before the holidays were to begin, a postcard from Billy was delivered at the cottage. Not many letters came there, and the receipt of the postcard was quite an event. The card merely gave Tom the date of Billy's arrival and stated that the first term had not been too bad, though he was looking forward to seeing Tom and to adventures in the forest.

38

Tom put the postcard in a book called *Coral Island*, which he had won as a school prize, handed to him by Lady Lander, who, as she did so, tried to pretend that this schoolboy was unknown to her. But Tom, whose eyes missed nothing, saw her lips twitch, and he felt the little push which she gave while handing him the prize. It was as good as a dig in the ribs, a touch of friendly conspiracy, that made the book all the more valuable.

So was the postcard valuable: a small matter, but it sent Tom out that Saturday morning as though he were riding a horse instead of trudging to the village by the sea, shopping basket in hand, on an errand for his mother.

It was already Christmas weather, with a leaden sky and a northeasterly wind blowing off the land out to a leaden sea. A few flakes of snow began to fall as Tom turned seaward off the lane, at the junction of the two roads, up that leading to the village. The big house which Billy had called the White Elephant stood back from the road where the lane ended. A tall hedge had been cut down, to expose the house, which was now very smart, newly painted, with black mortar between the brick-work and the window frames and front door gay with blue paint.

As Tom passed the gate leading into the drive, a girl came out, and seeing Tom, she smiled at him. He tried not to look at her, he was so embarrassed, but she walked alongside and spoke. "I saw you receive your prize yesterday. My stepmother and I were asked to the prizegiving at your school. I got home from my school two days ago—and without a prize."

She laughed, giving Tom a moment to notice how she had emphasized the "*step*mother". He registered that point and knew at once who she was. He did some more quick thinking, for much solitude may have made him shy, but not dull-witted. He was still suspicious of these people at the White Elephant. Harold Sims was one of them. So he said nothing.

The girl took no notice of his silence. "I'm going to the village," she said. "It's nice to have company."

"I'm the woodman's son," Tom said, rudely, by way of a challenge.

"I know you are," said the girl. "I've not had a chance to explore yet. I had to go off to school as soon as I got back from my summer holiday. But I'm longing to find my way around, especially in the woods."

"Can't your brother show you?" said Tom, more rudely still.

She looked at him for a moment before replying. She was puzzled by his hostility, for she knew nothing of his one contact with that brother.

"Oh," she said dryly, "he's my halfbrother. We've got the same father and the same name, but that's as far as it goes."

This cleared Tom's suspicion like sunlight from a misty morning. He dared to look at the girl and saw a thin figure, taller than himself, pale and dark. She looked sensible enough, almost like a woman, with thoughts of her own. She had been frowning when she last spoke, but now she smiled at him again, and this broke the ice. It almost made him reckless.

"Your brother shot down a thrush and let it get away wounded," he said, suddenly very passionate.

She was startled, too, and embarrassed. She evaded Tom's outburst, but it had brought them closer together.

40

"My name's Margaret," she said. "Known as Meg, though my mother didn't like that."

"Is she dead?" asked Tom, innocently.

Margaret didn't answer, and they walked on in silence for a while. The snow began to fall more fully, blowing like confetti from behind them and kissing them coldly on their necks as they faced the open country and the sea.

"It's coming," said Tom at last. "I'm sorry about that."

"Sorry about what?"

"Poking my nose in."

"Oh, that's nothing," she said. "It's not what people say, it's how they say it that matters. I don't think you could be mean."

This shattered poor Tom. He was not used to quick acquaintances. He belonged to the woodlands and the open air. Even in school he felt himself to be a foreigner and had made no friendships there.

He took a sidelong glance at the girl. She was staring ahead, quite calmly enjoying the sensation of the snow-flakes alighting on her face. It was a friendly face, patient and calm.

"You have to learn how to take people," she said. "I've had to, at any rate. There's my stepmother," she added, "and him."

"Who, your father?"

"No, Harold, who shot down the thrush."

"He was going to kill a robin, too."

"Why didn't he?"

"I stopped him. I knocked his arm down."

"Oh, dear," said Margaret, really alarmed. "He won't like you after that!"

This made Tom feel that he was in the right camp, and

he confided the tale of the poaching of the hare and the betrayal by Master Harold.

"I'm sorry," said the girl at the end of the story. "I don't understand him. What makes him like that, I wonder. His mother doesn't notice he's there most of the time, and when she does see him, she gives him every-thing he wants. It's like—it's like bribery."

"What about your father?" said Tom, now thoroughly at home with this girl who was almost a woman.

"Oh, he's busy making money."

That closed the confidence, for Tom and Margaret had reached the village, where the snow had begun to settle over the buildings and the highstreet. It was coming down thickly now and being blown aslant by the north-east wind, great billows of it dead white against the lead-colored sky.

"We shall have to face it, going back," said Tom, instantly abashed because he had suggested that they should walk back together.

But Margaret accepted this idea without saying a word. She told him what she had to do after posting letters, and

Tom left her at the grocery shop which was also the post office, while he went about his own errands.

They met again a quarter of an hour later and left the village, to take the road back inland against the snow, which was now a blizzard. They quickly became two specters, white from head to foot. Melting snow began to drip from Margaret's dark hair, making it heavy and still darker. Her pale cheeks were mottled by the battering of the flakes—their tiny but myriad hammerblows. So, too, with Tom. They looked at each other, leaning against the blizzard, and both laughed.

"Your eyelashes are white," said Margaret, and she put a gloved hand to her own eyes to clear the curtain that was blinding her.

They became more exposed when they reached the open country between the sea and the forest. After the baker's van passed them stumbling back to the village, the road was empty, and as they struggled on, they watched the track of the hooves and the wheels quickly filling up, leaving only a subpattern in the quilt of dull white, which now reflected the lifeless sky.

"This is fun," said Margaret. "But I'm glad I'm not alone, as I might have been."

Tom had nothing to say about that. He was hauling twelve pounds of flour in his basket and trying to keep it dry under a copy of the local newspaper, at which the wind snatched vindictively. The whole world was in a bad temper, except this stranger who struggled on beside him.

"You don't seem to mind rough weather," he shouted, to make himself heard above the howling of the wind through the branches of a twisted hawthorn which he and Margaret were passing.

"I'm used to rough weather," she said ruefully; and a grimace cracked the mask of snow on her face.

Tom knew what she meant and liked her all the more for it. But he did not follow this up, for once again there came an interruption from the world that was more familiar to him.

Running over the open country toward the shelter of the forest appeared the buck and doe, side by side, with the buck protecting his doe from the worst of the weather. They cut across the path of the two ghostly humans.

"Oh, look!" cried Margaret. "Look at them! Lovely! And see, she's carrying. She's all swollen up! Oh, the poor thing!"

"She don't worry," said Tom. "They are hardy enough. Our chaps drop bundles of hay around as soon as the snow comes. My dad will be out already, I expect."

"But she's carrying," repeated Margaret. There was a note of reverence in her voice. It made Tom turn his attention to her for a moment, bewildered by her excitement over something that was to him quite natural and to be expected. But he was watching the deer again as he replied, half abruptly, since all his interest was centered on the picture of the two graceful creatures moving silently, veiled in the snow-laden air, with the flakes disturbed by their movement swirling madly around them, like a solidification of their haughty breaths.

"Yes, they've been mated since last autumn. I've seen them about in the forest, since they left the rest of the herd. D'you see her, she's a lighter color than the others? She'd look almost white if it weren't for the snow."

Boy and girl stood still until they saw the couple diminish, to become mere shadows in the white darkness at midday, finally to melt into the further and solid darkness in the fringe of the forest.

The youngsters stood for a few moments, still spellbound by the apparition which had faded into the forest.

"You look as though you're asleep," said Margaret at last. "I've read about that!"

"Read about what?" said Tom, jerking himself back from the vision which had set him to daydreaming, as though seeking something which could never be found.

"About people dying in the snow. They fall asleep first."

Margaret was teasing him, a sure sign of liking, but Tom missed that. He was indignant.

"I wasn't," he said sharply, and began to walk on, crablike under the weight of the basket. Margaret was left half a pace behind, but with a double step she came abreast.

"You're too touchy," she said. "And that's what I wanted to say about my ferocious young brother. It's not altogether his fault."

But Tom could not understand this, and he trudged on in silence, with the girl beside him equally silent, because she feared he was a hopeless case.

When at last they reached the lane end and the gateway to the drive before the White Elephant, they paused for a second to examine each other, and what they saw made both of them laugh aloud: two white columns, crowned by two wet red faces, and eyes that glittered with warm life, after the fight against the blizzard.

Tom, to his surprise, found that the girl had been helping him carry the basket loaded with the package of flour. He had not noticed when she put a hand to it.

"Thanks," he said roughly.

"It's not your fault either," she said, and then she was gone.

45

7 Christmas Eve

Every year the Squire and his wife gave a Christmas party for neighbors, tenants and workers on the estate. It was held in the great hall, which was decorated with holly, mistletoe and a spruce tree in a cider barrel, the emblem of the season. Everybody received a gift from the pile of parcels heaped around the barrel.

Lady Lander, like her son, Billy, had a sense of humor and was tolerant of everybody, no matter how odd or unpleasant they might be. Sir George, more particular in his likes and dislikes, was dubious about inviting the newcomers from the White Elephant, the house which had been so difficult to dispose of because of its size. But it had been part of the estate for several generations, and the Squire was loyal to his ancestral properties. He had not liked Mr. Sims's drastic treatment of the house after buying it for less than it was really worth. A small fortune had since been spent on it, to make it look more conspicuous in the landscape and to modernize the interior.

Since the visit from Mrs. Sims and her son, Harold, soon after their settling in the renovated mansion, Sir George was still more wary of the whole family. The small

proposal "to be civil". So he lowered his hackles and greeted the newcomer politely.

The amicable consultation was interrupted by Arthur Winter, who had been indoors for a day or two after a slight accident. He had dropped a frosted log on his foot while taking fuel into the Hall.

He learned of the project to make a toboggan and at once took an interest in it.

"I got some strong planks back of the shop," he said and led the way behind the hut. He sent Tom back for a saw, hammer and nails and produced from his capacious pocket in the hip of his corduroy trousers a folded tapemeasure.

"Now you set about that," he said, pulling down a plank of wood some twelve feet long.

Under his guidance, the boys sawed four lengths, for runners and top. Then Arthur showed them how to cut triangular blocks on which to nail the sections together.

Hanging on the wall at the back of the shed were two iron felloes, rusty and long disused, taken from broken wagon wheels. Tom was sent to find a metal saw and pliers, and he and Billy cut the iron bands, not without difficulty, and Arthur instructed Harold (who hitherto had merely looked on) to hold the obstinately-coiled lengths of metal flat while the boys nailed them to the bottoms of the runners. This was a tedious job, for each nail hole in the bands had first to be punched. Harold sighed with boredom; but the others kept him to it, and he did not dare to revolt under the professional eye of Arthur Winter.

Half the morning had passed before the job was done, and then Arthur hobbled back indoors, chilled by enforced inaction.

"Now then," said Harold, "where do you and I try it out?"

Billy looked at him almost benevolently. "You mean the three of us?" he said.

"It won't hold more than two," said Harold.

"You're not as big as all that," said Billy. "We'll squeeze you into the middle. But first we want some guide ropes."

He looked at Tom, as though to say, "Now careful! Careful!" and Tom without a word disappeared again into the workshop to emerge with a length of rope, the ends of which he knotted over the protruding ends of the runners, where the wood had been trimmed away from the ground.

The boys dragged the toboggan out to the lane, which dropped downhill eastward away from the Hall. No traffic other than farm and forestry went that way, for the lane ended half a mile farther in a clearing where charcoal burning was carried on.

During the rest of the morning, amid the excitement of the successful runs on the toboggan, Billy had no opportunity to explain to Tom that Harold Sims had joined him purely by chance and was not particularly welcome. Indeed, he gave Tom the impression of enjoying the extra company and the close crowding of the three bodies on the toboggan, which caused Tom at the rear to cling to Harold Sims. This spoiled the morning's sport for him, though he did his best to disguise the fact and also his disappointment at not having Billy's undivided attention after the first long separation they had known.

But midday came, and with it a renewed fall of snow that began to fill up the ruts made by the toboggan down the slope to the charcoal burners' clearing.

"My word! It's Christmas Eve!" cried Billy as the boys dragged the toboggan through the cottage garden and left it tipped on end against the wall of the workshop. "Two days to the big party. Everybody comes to that, Sims. Your people had an invitation?"

"I wouldn't know," said Sims. "What d'you mean by everybody?"

Again Billy refused to be drawn. He said nothing and was too diplomatic even to look at Tom, though he knew this barb was directed at his friend.

But as Sims walked off, Billy lingered for a moment and spoke quietly to Tom. "Funny customer. Forced himself on me. Sorry about that, Tom. I'll be down alone before dark, unless you'd like to come up to the house and help with the decorations."

51

These words cleared the gloom of jealousy and anger which had threatened to darken Tom's pleasure in the morning's winter sport. He watched Billy join Harold Sims, who was waiting in the lane without having bidden Tom good-bye. It did not matter.

Tom did not go up to the Hall, but he was too restless to stay indoors waiting for Billy. He set off at three o'clock, choosing the woodland ride because the snow lay less thickly in the forest; but even so he had to stump along, lifting each leg laboriously step by step. His footprints were the only sign of human traffic along the path. The fall of snow at midday had not lasted, and fur and feather had been busy since then. The glistening surface was mottled with innumerable prints of pad and claw, and the white was discolored here and there with droppings, vivid yellow and brown crustings, sunk in the snow.

For some while Tom studied the tracks with interest, identifying the traffic: wood pigeon, tits, starlings, rooks, a fox, squirrels, and, in one closely marked track across the path, the hoofmarks of deer. Tom read these signs more knowledgeably than the pages of a book. They were his real scholarship, and for a while he gave himself up to this study with complete abandonment of every other interest.

But only for a while. Following the infinity of tracks, he found himself out at the edge of the woods. Ahead in the distance, at the end of a shallow dip in the open fields, he saw the eastern aspect of the Hall and the chimney stacks, outlined against the red sky, the rosy bricks still full of color from the sun setting in the southwest. Tom had no watch, but he knew the time by instinct. It would be about half past three.

But there was no sign of Billy.

Tom watched the sun gather pace and grow larger and redder, as it dropped toward the sea beyond the fields. The whole white stretch of open country flushed to red and held that richness for as long as the sun lingered. Then, as it changed from a full disk, to a half, to a rim, the cold rosy fire faded to violet, to blue, and nothingness.

Tom suddenly felt cold. Billy had said he would come, but he had not come. Tom might have gone on to the Hall. He had been invited. But instead, he turned back and began to pick his way, head downward, back through the woods, obstinately planting his feet in his own tracks. They seemed farther apart than his legs wanted to stretch now, on the return journey. Something had slowed him down.

But there was a compensation. As he turned at the bend, he saw something which he had not noticed on the way out.

The farmworkers responsible for feeding Sir George's herd of deer had dropped a truss of hay on the flat stump of the felled beech tree. It was one of a dozen or more, but the others were lying at intervals farther off, up the ride that ran straight on from the woodman's cottage into and through the heart of the forest.

Feeding from the isolated truss were the buck and the gray-coated doe. They stood side by side and were so hungry that they allowed Tom to approach. His bitter thoughts vanished. Slowly, step by step, he drew near, and still they went on tugging at the hay, mumbling little wisps and tossing their dainty heads as they ate.

Tom reached them and stood beside the doe. She shuddered, hesitated, looked sideways at him out of her

53

great startled eyes. She turned her head and went on eating. Tom gently put a hand on her flank and felt how hard and tense it was. Then, almost as an illusion, but yet a certainty, he felt a slight movement from within that swollen belly.

Quietly, he stepped backward and moved off toward home, leaving the pair of half-wild creatures to their winter meal. Darkness was creeping over the forest and the countryside, though the sky was still clear, and the moon, almost full, was gathering power southward over the sea. Tom was master again in his own kingdom.

8 The Party

Everybody came to a party on Boxing Day: neighboring squires and their families; the doctor, the vicar with theirs; the solicitor, a bachelor from the county town; no agent because Sir George was his own agent; every worker on the estate, including all the indoor servants, one of whom was Tom's aunt, his mother's sister who had lost her husband in the war in South Africa. Old hands and newcomers, none was forgotten.

Mrs. Winter made a great to-do of this every year, and each occasion meant an adaptation of her one party dress and a pressing of her two menfolks' Sunday clothes and a washing and ironing of shirts. She saw too that they had hip baths in the scullery, one after the other, with water heated in the copper. For in those days the Bible was obeyed in every detail, including the injunction "Thou shalt not look upon thy father's nakedness." So Arthur bathed first and was dispatched up to the front bedroom to dress, while Tom took his turn in the scullery.

The calm weather lasted over Christmas Day, which had been a quiet festival for the Winters, just themselves and the aunt from the Hall: not very lively for Tom, especially as he was in a subdued mood, for there had been no visit from Billy and no message from him. Also,

55

that incident in the forest on Christmas Eve remained in Tom's mind—something strange, some privilege to which he had been admitted. The way that doe had turned her head and looked at him, looked into his eyes, was something that haunted him, happily, with a kind of fierce pleasure that was almost painful.

The Winter family set off at six o'clock in the evening, leaving Caesar, the cat, to look after the cottage. Arthur put up a sheet of corrugated iron in front of the stove in the living room fireplace, propped up with the fire irons.

"That's safe enough," he said, taking up the storm lantern, which Tom had lighted, and ushering his wife and son out into the night. The countryside shone blue-cold, ghostly in the moonlight, which seemed to stand away from the small circle of buttercup yellow glow from the lantern.

Mrs. Winter was always nervous before these annual parties. "Now don't you say too much, Arthur," she said as they picked their way through the crisp snow along the lane. "And you, too, Tom! You mind your manners, and don't presume." What he was not to presume was left unsaid, for at the lodge gate by the drive up to the Hall, the Winters were joined by old Peter Apps and his wife, whose amiability drowned Mrs. Winter's anxiety.

The heavy oaken outer door of the Hall stood open on to the porch, which was already cluttered up with pairs of snow boots and galoshes. Beyond it, the inner glass-paneled door was on the latch. Through the panes the hall could be seen, the anteroom of hospitality, gay with holly and this new electric light. The Squire had installed it last autumn, with a donkey engine to feed the dynamo and batteries, somewhere among the kitchen premises. Its activity was marked by a faint throbbing sound which

56

provided a bass to all other domestic noises and the hum of conversation.

This party was the first full demonstration of the electric light, and nobody thought it odd when the light dimmed from time to time and then revived, as though the engine were taking a deep breath, returning to its task with renewed energy. A few oil lamps stood about, to augment the illuminations and add to the warmth from the great fire of logs hissing in the huge open fireplace, which had been in use for at least two hundred years.

Several tables, of differing heights, made a long buffet against one wall of the great hall, whose bare brick walls and high lancet windows suggested that the house was older even than the fireplace.

The buffet was loaded with Christmas fare, which attracted even more attention than the spruce tree at the other end of the hall, set in an angle between the entrance from the front hall and a door leading away into the interior. The tree was hung with spangles and crowned by a fairy doll with a little wand, whose star glittered and bobbed as the draft of air between the doors and the roaring fire stirred the twigs of the Christmas tree. A small mountain of parcels was piled around the tree, and outside that hovered the children of the estate like a flock of impatient sparrows.

The company was fully gathered by the time the Winters arrived. Mrs. Winter was always late because she "did not want to presume".

There was no formality. People just arrived, after dumping boots, cloaks, overcoats first in the entrance lobby and, when that was full, in two of the smaller rooms along the corridor, at the end of which stood the green baize-covered door that led to the kitchens.

The Sims family were last to arrive. Lady Lander saw them standing in the entrance hall after their carriage had driven away. "You didn't say what time we dined," said Mrs. Sims. "I'm afraid we're late."

Lady Lander touched her on the arm, and shook a number of bracelets which adorned it. "Oh, we're not dining," she said. "This is our free-for-all. Everybody comes, year after year. I hope you'll find people you've already met. It's rather a big family." Then she added, "But it *is* a family."

Mrs. Sims was an important-looking woman. She showed her husband's riches to advantage. The crowd in the great hall parted to make way for her as she sailed in, followed by Mr. Sims and Harold, both vividly groomed. Somewhere behind, and already parted from them by other people, came Margaret.

Tom saw her and was embarrassed when she saw him, too, and smiled, as she had done when they first met. Indeed, she looked no different, though dressed for the party. Her stepmother must have given up in despair, trying to smarten her: she might still have been going to post letters.

She began to make her way toward him, where he stood with his parents, who were at a loss what move to make next after being bold enough to join the crowd. Tom saw Harold Sims look around at his halfsister and jerk his head irritably, as though commanding her to keep up with her family, which was heading for Sir George Lander, who stood talking with two other gentlemen between the Christmas tree and the fireplace.

But Margaret ignored this command. She reached the Winters and spoke to Mrs. Winter. "I envy you, Mrs. Winter, living on the edge of the forest. That's just what

58

I'd like. But still, we are not far away, and I want to explore there. You will be guide, won't you, Tom?"

She told Mrs. Winter about the walk to the village, and was so friendly and easy that the good woman forgot about the danger of "presuming" and found herself talking freely with the girl, not even weighing up her own impression of this newcomer against that given by Tom when he had described the stranger who had accompanied him to the village.

Margaret was equally easy with Billy Lander who joined the Winter family as soon as he saw them in the crowded hall. "I couldn't get out after all," he said to Tom. "Mother wanted help with the parcels." He nodded his head toward the pile around the Christmas tree. "But I knew you would understand."

But Tom was not prepared to understand. All he knew was that after only one term away at school his friendship with Billy appeared to be growing cool, as he had feared it would. So he said nothing and gave the impression of being sulky.

This left Margaret and Billy to talk together, and finally to wander away toward the tables laden with cold turkey, rounds of beef, meat pies, salads, mince pies, jellies and blancmanges, a cask of beer and a platoon of wine bottles with their corks drawn. The indoor servants helped guests who were shy or awkward, but they too were guests tonight and helped themselves to food along with the rest of the crowd. Even Jeremy Hogg came off his high horse and could be seen, plate in hand, circulating good-humoredly. He even waited on Mrs. Winter, a condescension which almost put her into a flurry again, after she had been reassured by the friendly talk with Margaret Sims.

59

So Tom and his father were left standing together, but not for long, because Arthur saw Peter Apps drawing tankards of ale from the barrel and setting them in regimental order beside it, each one capped with a nice head of froth. And the meat pies were being portioned out onto plates, to form another appetizing regiment.

"Well, I don't know," said Arthur aloud, only half addressing himself to Tom. "But I fancy a round of that pie. Ain't you hungry yourself, Tom?"

He did not wait for an answer. Tom saw him making for that table like a cat stalking a bird.

The boy was now left alone; and to be alone in a crowd is to be doubly alone. He stood there, disconsolate and still angry.

"Why, young Tom Winter, you be making no progress." It was Peter Apps, hardly recognizable in a black Sunday suit, an awkward substitute for his workaday outfit of fustian coat, breeches and leather leggings. "You follow your dad's example, lad, and get a good helping. Even a sup of that mild beer will do you no harm. Proper hangdog, you look. What's gotten into you, boy?"

This was said heartily, for Peter Apps was in his third tankard, and he carried a second helping of roast turkey.

"I'm not hungry," said Tom.

"Why, are you sickening?"

"I'm all right," said Tom, more obstinate than ever.

"A fellow who can't come to the table won't be all right. If you be so, then you should eat."

So Tom, to avoid being taken more notice of, followed his father and collected a plateful of meat pie. He took no beer, and shrank into a corner where he tried to eat. But he had already supped too well on his grievance, and the food almost choked him.

60

Nor was he left alone for long. Lady Lander, who was circulating serenely among the guests, approached him. "Why, Tom, how nice to see you! We've missed you here since Billy went to school. You should have come in sometimes to borrow a book. You still enjoy reading, do you not? How is it at school?"

She jockeyed him along, and he found himself helping the indoor staff to carry further helpings to older folk who were sitting against the walls, waiting to be fed.

Then something happened. Tom found himself face to face with Harold Sims. This young gentleman had been doing well at the table. He was about to return there with an empty plate. Instead, he held out the plate to Tom and said, with an impersonal air as though addressing a waiter, "Take this back, and bring me a mince pie."

Behind him stood his halfsister, Margaret, talking and eating with Sir George and Billy. They must have overheard, for Harold's voice was a carrying one, cold and clipped.

Poor pent-up Tom, still brooding over his troubles, could contain himself no longer. With a sharp blow of his fist, he knocked the plate out of Harold's hand. It shattered on the floor.

Too much noise was going on in the hall for any but the nearby people to hear the crash or to notice the two boys, the one cold and amused, the other scarlet with rage.

Sir George had seen. He took Tom by the arm and said, "Come with me."

They disappeared through the door leading farther into the house, and Tom found himself in Sir George's study-office, whose French doors gave on to a gravel sidewalk and a view across the gardens to the forest, with a couple of fields between the Hall and the trees.

The room was in darkness, except for the glow from a coal fire. Sir George did not switch on the electric light.

"That was deliberate bad temper, young man. What have you got to say for yourself? You were in good company, and this is Christmastide. You were my guest, Tom. It's a bad business."

Tom had sobered down. He was bitterly mortified and in terror lest his mother had witnessed his outburst of temper.

"That's not the reason," he said.

"It certainly was not. There was no reason whatever in your conduct. I heard what young Sims said to you. He was being unpleasant. You fell into the trap, Tom Winter. You are not usually such a fool."

Sir George looked at him, pondering for some moments.

"You had better wait in here for a while, to think things out—whether it is worthwhile to lose control of yourself. Look at that clock." He pointed at the mantelpiece, where the French clock was flanked by letters wedged between it and two opposing bronze statuettes of deer.

"It is a quarter to seven, and the evening is young. When it strikes seven, come out again and rejoin the party. I'll leave you to yourself—and your common sense."

Tom was left alone. He could hear the distant roar of human voices, but it meant nothing to him. He was still enraged and struggling to control that rage. And he was bewildered. Sir George had made him feel ashamed, and shame was fighting a battle with anger, wild and

63

violent, though the boy stood as still as a statue, clear in the moonlight that flooded in through the French doors, brighter than the warm glow from the coal fire.

The minutes passed, but Tom did not move. He stood with his fists clenched. His throat ached. But he did not give way, nor was he thinking. He just stood there at the center of the conflict within him, hopeless and humiliated.

Then a movement outside drew his mind back to earth, to something other than himself.

He moved closer to the French doors and peered into the other world, the white and shadowy world of moonlit snow. Beyond the lawn immediately outside the house, a band of darkness indicated a sunk fence; beyond it the meadow lay under an unsullied quilt of snow, which broke the moonlight up, blues, yellows, grays. Beyond that, the forest was dark, an impenetrable mass.

But out of it two figures had appeared, and they now moved nervously toward the sunk fence.

Tom lost his troubles. The storm within him died away. He did not hear the clock strike seven in a little silvery voice. He was watching the buck and doe, moving with them in his imagination, nervous as they, anxious for them. He knew they were looking for food, seeking it from the great house, tamed by their hunger.

They were beautiful in the moonlight, like fairy creatures, liable to vanish as dreams vanish. Tom was so entranced that he did not hear the door behind him open, was not aware that Billy Lander had entered the room and had shut the door quietly.

Billy crept closer and saw what Tom was staring at. But he saw more. He saw Tom also, whom he had expected to find lost in misery.

"Are you all right?" he whispered.

Tom started, but his attention was still fixed on the scene outside. "Look," he said, "Look, Billy."

The tone of his voice was so commanding that Billy said no more. He saw Tom lost in worship. So they stood, while the deer reached the sunk fence, to be halted there and to turn, hesitantly, then move away, back across the meadow, to disappear into the darkness of the forest. Only the tiny hoofprints remained, punctuating the smooth surface of the snowfield with points of shadow.

9   A Truce

"Was Father pretty fierce with you?" said
Billy, after the disappearance of the deer broke the spell,
and Tom had recovered from his trance. The question
made Tom realize how kindly he had been handled by
the Squire.

"No, he wasn't," he said. "But I don't want to go
back."

"Don't be a fool, Tom."

"That's what your father said. He called me a fool
because I fell into the trap. What did he mean?"

Billy pondered, then answered thoughtfully, "Can't
you see? Young Sims is trying to beat you down because

you stopped him at his little game the first time you met. He's as cussed as you are."

Tom said nothing. He couldn't understand this explanation. Billy dropped his manner of serene good temper and spoke with uncharacteristic emphasis. "Look here, Tom. Sims has come to live here, and we've got to be civil. I told you so before, but you're still as stuck up as he is. You've nothing to lose by treating him decently. It would be more to your credit, whatever he does. We've got to teach him our ways. He's a town boy, and a spoiled one at that. He'll learn, if you don't ride him at every turn."

"But why does he try to put me down?"

Billy could not reply because Sir George came in. "Well, Tom, it's struck seven, and you've not returned."

He put a hand on Tom's shoulder. "Don't forget, Tom, that I heard what provoked you. Let's get back to the party . . . after the accident. That's what it was, Tom—an accident, eh?"

Then he added, "You might as well explain it that way to young Sims. His sister has taken him aside and had a few words with him. A nice girl, that. He could follow her example."

Tom walked meekly after Sir George, followed by Billy, who prodded him affectionately in the back.

"Go to it, idiot," whispered Billy as they plunged into the hurly-burly and din of the party, now in full swing under the influence of the plentiful food and drink. The village schoolmaster, a good musician, was sitting at the grand piano, reveling in the touch of a noble instrument, and some of the tenants were beginning to dance.

Sir George left the boys and partnered Mrs. Sims, expecting that Mr. Sims would take Lady Lander, but

67

Mr. Sims was busy talking politics or business with two gentlemen near the buffet. He was laying down the law about something and ignored the opportunity to add to the happier proceedings of the Christmas party.

To Tom's amazement, he saw Lady Lander take his father by the arm and lead him on to the center of the floor, where a space had been cleared for dancing. And Arthur responded gallantly, dancing with no little skill, under the anxious eye of his wife, who was overcome by the distinction given to her man.

"There you are, you see," said Billy to Tom, indicating his mother and Tom's father so easily paired in the dance. He spoke as though clinching an argument, though there had been no argument. But Tom was reassured. He was still under the healing influence of that spectacle from the French doors of the study—the silence of it, the gentle confidence of those two creatures approaching the house and withdrawing so peacefully, their serenity undisturbed by finding nothing to eat and the ditch preventing their further approach.

Margaret Sims met the boys.

"How long before we can do some exploring, Billy?" she said, and as she spoke, she took Tom by the arm. "I'm longing to see everything, the forest, the farms, the beach. Don't forget these are my first days here. You both must know every inch."

"We'd better go down to the shore while the snow's about," said Billy, grateful for her help in bringing Tom Winter back into circulation. "Why not tomorrow?"

"We'll all be in bed in the morning," said Margaret. "It looks as though the party is only just beginning, and we'll be home late. Why not make it afternoon?"

Billy agreed. Tom felt his arm being shaken as

Margaret spoke to him. "And you, too, Tom? You'll come, won't you? I'll have to ask Harold. We can't leave him out, for he knows nobody here yet."

Tom nodded. He still could not speak. But that was enough for Margaret. She led him away toward the buffet, and Billy followed. There they found Harold. He and Tom looked at each other.

"Nobody's sorry," said Harold, and he gave Tom a sour smile. His sister's talk had not had much effect.

"I don't know," said Tom. He was not sure what he meant by that, but it was as near as he could get to an apology.

The three young people set to and had a good supper, though Harold by this time had got to the ice-cream stage. His appetite had not been in the least disturbed by the incident which had upset Tom Winter so deeply.

10 Down by the Sea

Margaret was right. The party had lasted until midnight, by which time feet were weary and the buffet tables as empty as though the locusts had swept over them.

Up at the Hall and at the White Elephant, everybody lay abed until late in the morning. The countryfolk on the farms and around the estate, however, were up and about as usual. In the woodman's cottage Mrs. Winter had her household stirring before daylight, for her conscience troubled her after so much pleasuring over the Christmas holiday. She saw the clear sky and the glittering stars through the casement window when she was wakened by the premature crowing of the cock in the hen roost.

"Arthur, there be a fox about, to set that cock crowing in the dark."

This woke Arthur, and his stirring woke Tom in the back room. They all got up, Mrs. Winter setting about preparations for washing day, before getting the breakfast. She was bright enough after the party and still purring at the friendly notice taken of her little family up at the Hall and of the fact that "there had been no difference made", as she said.

"What's got you, Mother?" Arthur laughed. "You talk that old-fashioned. Things is on the move nowadays, woman. One man's as good as another, I reckon."

Mrs. Winter was deeply shocked. "You say such things, Arthur, and in front of the boy, too. He wants no encouraging that way."

Tom wondered what more she would have said had she known of the unfortunate encounter with Harold Sims at the party, though he knew that she did not extend her humility to rich townfolk. They belonged to a world beyond her understanding.

Tom was happy this morning. Everything looked as bright as the sunrise, which dawned across the breakfast table from the southeast, where open country sloped toward the cliffs and the sea. The stars paled and vanished, and out of a low belt of violet mist the sun drew itself up, crimson and pear-shaped, then a perfect sphere of glimmering fire, risen triumphant, too bright to be seen.

By midday the snow over the open scrubland was steaming, a faintly visible translation from solid to vapor. The sunlight touched the forest also, creating movement there, loosening snow from the laden boughs and letting it slide to the ground, with a sound of shuffling and thudding, the branches then released rising to their normal

71

position, and shining wet and black against those still laden.

Mrs. Winter was washing the dishes after the midday meal when Billy Lander knocked at the back door. She opened it, and in rushed Pembroke, the corgi, wagging his tailless rump and causing Caesar, the cat, to leap up to the dresser and glower balefully from that safe retreat.

"Hello, Mrs. Winter, am I too early for Tom?"

"That you aren't, Master William. He's chopping some kindling out in the shed. I wonder he didn't see you, coming in by the back way."

"Yes, I walked through the woods. The snow is still firm there, and I saw a fox run across."

"Ah! We must watch the hens tonight, I reckon. I'll put Arthur on to it."

"There's not much he doesn't know about the woods, eh, Mrs. Winter?" said Billy. "I'll bet he was talking about his trees to my mother when she was dancing with him last night!"

"No, he wouldn't have done that, Master William, though he's that forward at times. I wouldn't have Tom catch that from him."

"Oh, Tom! He's too much the other way, though he can break out occasionally."

Billy was tempted to tell Mrs. Winter of Tom's two attacks on Harold Sims, but he thought better of it.

"I'll go and pick him up," he said. "We've planned to take the Simses down to the beach. That girl is keen to explore. She'll soon know as much about our land as Tom does. Come on, Pembro!"

The corgi needed no second bidding. He was out instantly, barking down the garden, and Caesar relaxed,

72

but cautiously remained on the dresser until absolutely reassured.

Billy found Tom in the shed, chopping up small logs into kindling sticks.

"I'm ready," said Tom. "Didn't hear you come until Pembro barked."

"I looked indoors for you and have had a talk to your mother."

"You didn't say anything?"

Billy looked at Tom almost with disgust. "What is the matter with you? You're suspicious of your own shadow. Can't you live a bit easier, Tom?"

"Well, I don't know," said Tom, dubiously.

"Come on now," said Billy, "or we shall lose the daylight. I came for you first, didn't I? I might have met you with the others, less far to go!"

Tom appreciated this. He put on his coat, and the boys set off by the front gate and the lane toward the big house, where they were to meet Margaret and Harold.

Margaret stood alone at the entrance to the drive of the White Elephant. She wore an old mackintosh and thick shoes and had a red woolen scarf wound around her neck.

"Harold says he will follow us," she said, after greeting the boys.

"What, is he still in bed?" said Billy.

"You mean recovering from the feast?" said Margaret, and she laughed, but it was a hollow laugh.

Where the forest lane met the road to the village, a footpath led from a stile across the open country. It was now merely a dent in the unbroken stretch of snow.

"You lead, Tom," said Billy. "He's the trusty guide, Margaret. Follow him to the end of the world, and you'll arrive safely."

73

It was good to hear the girl laugh. She seemed to break out, like a butterfly from a chrysalis, and to spread her wings in the sunlight and warmth.

"You're a nice pair!" she said, taking her place in the single file between the two boys. "I wish I'd brought a stick. I'm not used to floundering about in the unknown."

"Grab at Tom if you fall into a rabbit hole. It's too late now to cut you a stick; nothing but twisted hawthorns down to the cliff top."

They had not gone far into the scrubland when they heard a shout from the stile. Pembroke leaped around and barked, pointing at the stile. He was in a state of happy delirium and had been burrowing with his muzzle through the untrodden snow. A clot of it had gathered between his ears, a white bonnet on his golden head.

But his pleasure was interrupted. With an ugly growling and snorting, Harold's new acquisition, a large Airedale, came bounding along, and, before his master had left the stile, was level with the others, and instantly it attacked the corgi, who howled and rolled over on his back.

Margaret at once pounced, to seize the Airedale by the collar, but she could not bring him off. He shook her about as he tried to get Pembroke by the throat.

"Let go!" cried Billy. "He'll turn on you."

And he seized the girl around the waist, while Tom Winter turned and took the Airedale from behind, by the collar which Margaret had relinquished. He was quite calm. He leaned over and spoke to the dog and put a hand on its head between the ears.

"That's it! That's it now, good boy," he whispered, while Billy secured Pembroke, who had miraculously been released, and took him up in his arms, whence the

74

surprised little Welshman rumbled with indignation but
was unharmed.

Harold now arrived. "Fierce little brutes, those cor-
gis," he gasped, short of breath after floundering through
the snow. "Is it your dog?" He spoke to Tom.

"No, Pembroke belongs to me." Billy was white in the

face. For once, he was angry and fighting to control
himself. "Your hound leaped on him from behind. He
was leading us quietly enough."

Harold hesitated. Then he changed his tactics.

"Oh, I'm sorry," he said. "Mine's new. He's not
trained yet. I've got to train him for hunting."

"For *what*?" said Billy, astounded.

But Harold let that drop. He had not, until this
moment, noticed that his dog was standing docilely
beside Tom, who still had him by the collar. "That's all
right, Winter," said the owner. "You can let him go."

75

"Then it's onward march," said Margaret, who was quite undisturbed. But she had noted Tom's touch of magic with the Airedale.

For a short way Billy carried Pembroke, until he was assured that the other dog was under control. Who was responsible for that control it was difficult to say, but the animal remained interested in Tom, walked beside or around him, and returned to him after every bout in advance of the party. He took no further notice either of his master or the corgi, after Billy had decided to trust Pembroke to freedom again. But now the Welshman was inclined to become the aggressor, growling in a most menacing undertone whenever the Airedale crossed his path or was inclined to be playful.

Billy Lander was quiet, watchful. He, rather than Tom, was distrustful of Harold. Tom apparently had not noticed how the Airedale's owner had tried to fasten the blame on him again. The law of nature, an overwhelming passion, took hold of Tom immediately he was confronted with animals or any wildlife of fur, feather or foliage. It gave him a quality of authority. Even Harold Sims was impressed and did not care to show his jealousy or possessiveness over his own dog.

The party of four humans and two dogs plowed its way across the open country toward the sea, leaving a fine confusion of footprints along the indentation which marked the hidden footpath. The sunshine picked out the colors of the garments and the dogs' coats, doubling their intensity by contrast with the glare of the snow, whose surface was melting and refreezing, as the heat of the sun played on it from above and the icy cold from below.

"What do we do when we get there?" asked Harold.

"We shall just be there," said Billy coldly. Sims appeared to be subdued. He was perhaps awed by the Squire's son and was clever enough to realize that he had made a mistake in opening yet another attack on Tom Winter, whose friendship with Billy Lander completely puzzled him.

"It was your idea, wasn't it?" said Margaret to Billy. "Something always happens where the sea meets the land."

"That sounds like a quotation," said Billy, a little more warmly. He found it astonishing that this girl and Harold could be blood relations. "Are you a blue stocking?"

"I don't know what I am," said Margaret.

"Nor does anybody else," said Harold.

"I should say you were a lucky devil," said Billy.

Harold laughed. It sounded like breaking glass.

Tom missed this conversation, for he had pushed on ahead. He was content to be alone with the unusual aspect of things, the world under snow. He was happier today. The incident at the party had brought no apparent consequences. Everything was transformed by the glory of the sunshine on the snow. He was in his own world, and this success in making an instant mastery over Harold Sims's savage dog gave him renewed confidence.

Tom was first to the end of the footpath, which led to a gully through the high cliff, outlet of a small stream which had broken away from the main estuary beyond the village farther west. It was an isolated place, and the gully sloped fairly steeply down, narrow and crowded with thorn trees, elder and tamarisk, to open on the strip of sandy beach, now snow-clad. The bushes and the tufts of dead grasses were hummocks under the snow, and the descent was treacherous because of the uncertain depth of the snow, step by step. Once the corgi disappeared suddenly as he breasted a smooth patch between two draped bushes. Billy lifted him out of a concealed rabbit burrow, Pembroke yelping with excitement meanwhile, moved to frenzy by the scent.

Margaret was the first to break out of the gully. She also nearly broke her neck, for excited by the joy of coming out to the open beach and the sea, she threw up her arms, as though to embrace the universe, and began to dance.

But she chose the wrong spot. She was dancing on thin ice, where the stream had spread out into the sand. The surface of this deeply saturated sand was frozen and bore a deceptive coating of snow. Margaret's little ballet was too heavy for that unruffled floor. She broke through up to her knees and toppled over.

"Don't come! Don't come!" she shouted. "You'll all fall in, too."

But Billy was already spread-eagled on the snowfield beside her, reaching out his arms. "Don't flounder about," he said. "You'll soak yourself and freeze to death."

"Idiot!"

"No! I'm just reaching you. Hook onto me and ease yourself up slowly."

Tom Winter approached from the other side and followed Billy's example. Margaret reached out her arms, and, supported by both boys, was able to lever herself up, gingerly raising her legs and stepping forward and then aside to firm ground.

Her brother, meanwhile, had walked on alone down the beach, calling his dog, not looking back once to see if his sister were in danger. "We shall have to keep on the move, or you really will freeze up," said Billy.

"Thank you both," said Margaret. "No bones broken. But I couldn't have got out alone without a complete soaking."

All three ran down the beach after Harold, Pembroke struggling bravely behind, handicapped by his short legs, barking loudly in protest. This excited the Airedale, who began barking also and racing to and fro over the untouched level, scattering snow, and creating a confusion of tracks.

Suddenly he stopped dead, turned abruptly, and pointed.

There, far ahead of the party, which like the Airedale had come to a halt and to silence, a large hare sat on the beach, almost at the water's edge, staring out to sea. It was upright, on its haunches, with its forepaws held up together as though in prayer. The long ears lay back, and though the animal was some distance away, Tom's keen eyes saw those of the hare; saw the gleam in them of reflected fire from the sunset out of the sea.

Tom was quite unaware that Margaret was watching him as he stood spellbound.

One second, two seconds passed, everything and everybody motionless, the glow of the sunset coloring all with unreality.

Then, with a wolflike howl, the Airedale sprang forward. The cry acted strangely on his master, Harold Sims. The boy became demented, he cried out, in a shrill piping voice, "At him, boy! At him!" and began to flounder madly along the snow-clad beach.

Before Tom could move, he found himself clasped by Billy. "Don't, don't, Tom! It's safe enough. They can't possibly reach it. Look! There you are. He's spotted them! He's off like a streak of lightning!"

Tom was trembling. He tried to break away from Billy's grasp. But Margaret, too, was concerned. She pointed ahead and touched Tom with her other hand. "Look, it's gone! It's safe, Tom! They can't touch it!"

The hare had doubled back up the beach and disappeared beyond some loose rocks, probably into a cave entrance in the cliff. But the Airedale followed, giving voice loudly. His bark echoed from the overtowering cliff above and was lost out to sea. He rooted about unseen for some time, his voice muffled by distance and the disposition of the rocks.

Some ten minutes later, Harold, who had disappeared too, returned, followed by the Airedale. "Lost it!" he said. His face was flushed, his eyes feverish. "What a chase!"

The others were silent. He looked from one to the other, surprised. Then his excitement died away. He frowned, bewildered by something he could not understand.

"I'm going back," he said. "It'll be dark before we hit the road."

11 An Accident

The frost continued, and also the fine weather, with eight hours of winter sunshine from rise to fall, the snow melting on the surface each day and freezing again at night, gradually consolidating on the ground and glassing everything upright with icicles: roofs, windows, branches. The landscape became a world in aspic.

"I reckon we'll take down that other oak which Mr. Hogg marked," said Arthur Winter to Tom. "Do you good to have a job of work. Waste of time, all these school holidays, eh, Mother?"

"He's been at his books, hasn't he?" said Mrs. Winter.

"Books!" Arthur sniffed. "That don't do his limbs much good. Living on dreams, that is; all this reading!"

Tom was used to this argument between his parents. It left him untouched. He knew how far to go with both of them, and that was a good way, full of trust, deep beneath his mother's anxieties and his father's easy outlook, somewhat too easy, because of his good nature.

"Billy was coming for me this morning," said Tom.

"What to do?"

"Oh, just exploring."

"What, traipsing about in idleness, up to any mischief?"

"Stop that teasing, Arthur," said Mrs. Winter. "Always on at the boy, you are."

Arthur chuckled and looked affectionately across the breakfast table at his son. "Well, a morning with the ax won't come amiss to either of you. I reckon young Billy will take to that."

"You're sure there's no danger for him, Arthur? We'd never hear the last of it if anything happened."

Arthur ignored this. He had lived with it for over fourteen years. As he got up from the table, there was a commotion outside the front door, followed by a vigorous knock. Mrs. Winter opened the door, to admit Billy Lander, Pembroke and Margaret Sims.

The girl looked inquiringly at Mrs. Winter.

"Do you mind?" she said. "Billy came for Harold, but Harold's in bed. He caught a chill that day we went down to the beach, though I was the one who got wet feet!"

"So I've brought her along," said Billy to Tom.

82

"Just as well," said Arthur. "Tom's got a job of work this morning. We're bringing down another oak and cleaning both up."

"Oh!" cried Margaret. "Wonderful! I must come. I want to help. I've never seen a tree felled."

"It's a sad sight," said Mrs. Winter. "All that life coming to an end."

But nobody heeded her. Arthur was willing to enlist all three youngsters, and they followed him in great excitement to the outhouse, where he selected the tools for the job: the double-handed saw, three smaller saws, a long-handled heavy ax, a pick, chisels, a chopper, a hone and the coils of rope.

"We'll bring some sacking to stand on," he said. "Snow gets that mucky underfoot when you tread it around."

Margaret carried the sacks and found them heavier than she expected before the expedition had gone far along the forest ride. After so many days since the fall, the snow was pockmarked and in places glassy with the noontide thaw and the night's refreezing.

"Mind how you pick your way," said Arthur, who was in front. "Don't want to slip with these tools in your hands."

The youngsters trod with deliberate care, avoiding the glassy patches.

Billy looked up at the glazed trees. "It'll be like bringing down a glass chandelier," he said. "Tinkle! Tinkle!"

The doomed oak glittered in the early sunlight. Its forest companion which Arthur and Tom had felled before Christmas, lay near it, pointing toward a clump of smaller wood, now set almost solid in refrozen snow.

"I ain't too happy," said Arthur. "Pretty slippery business, it be."

83

"Oh, let's start. I can't wait!" cried Margaret, as eager as she had been that day when she began to dance on the beach.

"You stand back, missy, and mind you do as I bid when we come to the downfall. You shall help, but this part be man's work."

Margaret pouted and appealed to Tom, who was preparing the ropes, but Billy intervened. "It really is risky, Margaret. That's why we have to rope the tree, to make it fall the way we want. But there's always the odd chance."

"Not if I'm careful," she said. "Why do you all think girls are harebrained?"

"I don't think so at all, but you're inclined to rush things. Look at what happened the other day, when you danced on thin ice!"

"Oh," she cried, "you wise old man! You ought to grow a beard. Tom wouldn't say that to me, would you, Tom?"

But Tom was already at work with his father, dealing with the ropes. The tree trunk was unclimbable, coated with ice. Arthur tied a stone to the rope end and flung it up over an upper branch. Then he made a slipknot and drew it up securely against the branch, Tom hauling with him. This was repeated with a second rope, and the two were then drawn tight, at a right angle from each other, and pegged to the ground with the help of the pick and the cold chisels. This would ensure that the oak must fall as near as maybe alongside the first one, without damaging any neighboring wood.

The job was tough, for the frozen ground was brittle, and tools slipped.

"Now then," said Arthur, "we might begin."

But he took a walk round the fettered tree, measuring with shrewd glances upward and around him, taking note of the clearance.

"That be fair enough, I reckon," he said. Then he studied the youngsters for a moment, looking from one to another appraisingly. "So you be set on taking a hand?" he said to Margaret. " 'Tis not ladies' work."

"Oh, please, don't start all that again," cried Margaret. "I'm as tough as these boys and two years older."

"And a proper woman, too, I'd say. But you must wait till we've brought him down. Then you can help saw the branches. 'Tisn't proper you should use a chopper. They be dangerous things with all this ice about."

Margaret had to be content with that, and she stood back for a while, to watch the skillful way in which Arthur chipped a groove into the bole of the oak, for the ax to bite. Then he took one handle of the big saw and put the two boys to the other, and the slow progress began, back and forth, back and forth.

After five minutes Arthur stopped. "We'll draw a breath, lads."

He also took another look around at the ropes. "That be well set," he said and returned to his end of the saw. Tom and Billy, both flushed, bent to the task. Margaret, urged by curiosity, crept nearer, several paces, but still well away from the scene of action.

The steady rhythm was resumed, its hoarse music as regular as the ticking of a grandfather clock, but long drawn out, rasping on the quiet of the snow-quilted woods. Then another pause, and a resumption of the steady labor.

The vibration brought down patches of frozen snow from the boughs above and an occasional sliver of ice that tinkled and shattered around the foot of the tree. Laughter broke from the three mortals when one of them was caught by this icy shower.

Margaret studied every detail. She was so entranced by the work and the initial indifference of the tree that she did not notice how she was creeping, gradual pace by pace, nearer and nearer to the carpet of sacks where Arthur, Tom and Billy were crouched.

The sun had risen a little higher, and shafts of light penetrated to the floor of the forest, making patches of moisture where the frozen snow melted on the surface. Some of the stuff dislodged from the tree was watery, too, and this gave the effect of sweat. It was the oak's death sweat.

Margaret was now near enough to smell the sawdust: the sharpness of it, almost acrid and musty. She saw the topmost boughs trembling and flakes of snow like butterflies, dark against the blue sky, fluttering off and falling.

"I'll take another look," said Arthur, releasing the saw and putting a hand to the small of his back. "Getting near his time now, lads, so keep a look out and be smart when I shout."

He walked around the tree and was so concentrated on his examination that he included Margaret in his circle without noticing her.

"Well, now," he said, "this be the last turn, Tom. Watch out, Master William. Won't do for you to come to grief. When I shout, back you jump."

They set to again, and after a few minutes the same process began. The oak groaned and swayed, then seemed to try to recover its ancient dignity. The sawing went on.

"Now, boys, back!" shouted Arthur.

But at that instant, the cold chisel holding down the rope toward the boys' side of the tree pulled out of the slippery ground. The tree creaked, swayed, and, held by only the one rope near Arthur, crashed at an angle. A large lower branch caught him and brought him to the ground.

For a second Margaret and the boys stood paralyzed. Margaret was the first to act. "Tom, Tom!" she cried. "Your father!"

She ran forward, ducking under the branch, and reached down to the figure seemingly crushed beneath it. "Quick," she cried, "saw this branch away."

She knelt above Arthur, pressing up with her hands while Tom and Billy sawed through the branch. Their effort seemed interminable, but at last they were through and also easing the branch away from Arthur, with Margaret steering it from beneath.

It had grazed Arthur's face, which was bleeding, and Margaret saw that his arm was doubled back, broken. Tom knelt beside him, stanching the blood from his cheek.

"I'll go for help," said Billy. "Home's the nearest. We'll bring a stretcher."

He ran off, and Tom and Margaret were left alone with the injured man, both of them too filled with dread to be able to speak. But Arthur was tough. After some minutes he regained consciousness and opened his eyes.

"That blasted rope gave," he muttered, "blasted rope." Then he groaned, tried to move, and shouted with pain.

"Still! Lie still, Mr. Winter," whispered Margaret. "We don't know what it is. Billy has gone for help. We'll soon get you home."

87

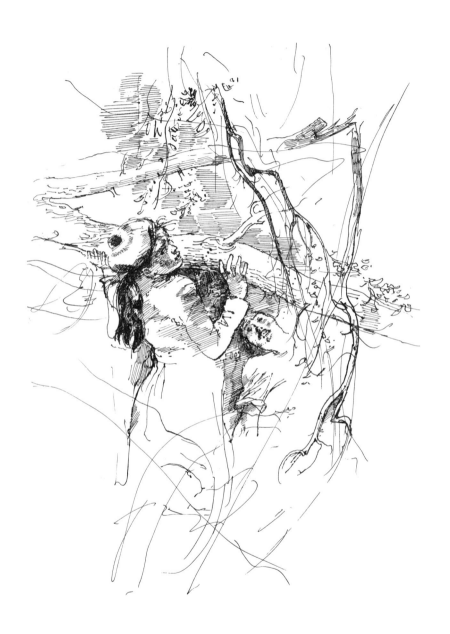

"I be that cold," said Arthur. "Could do with a pint of ale."

Tom fetched his jersey and put it under his father's head. Margaret, who was wearing a wool-lined mackintosh, took it off and laid it over Arthur.

"Try not to move," she said. "We mustn't move you until the doctor comes."

"That be damned," said Arthur. "I want to get to me bed."

"It's all right, Tom," said Margaret. "I'm sure there's nothing hurt inside. But his arm is broken. I wish they'd hurry."

But they had to wait for a quarter of an hour before they heard the sound of human voices. It was a long quarter of an hour, a dreadful silence lay over it, except for the drip, drip of melting snow and an occasional whine from Pembroke, who knew by dog-wisdom that something was wrong.

At last Billy appeared, leading Sir George and three men, with a stretcher.

"What's this, Winter?" said the Squire severely. He was deeply concerned. "We'd better wait," he said. "Not safe to move him until the doctor comes." He took off his overcoat and laid it on top of Margaret's.

"What made him choose a day like this?" he asked, addressing himself to nobody in particular. "Tom, you'd better go home and prepare your mother," he said.

"I'm not leaving my dad," muttered Tom, who was still kneeling by his father, holding a handkerchief to the wound in Arthur's cheek.

"I'll go," said Margaret.

"Oh, you are here? Yes, a good idea; don't make too much of it."

"I know what to do, Sir George," said Margaret with such dignity that he looked at her with respect.

"Right, young woman," he said. "Thank you. Yes, I believe you."

Then he turned to his son. "Billy, while we are waiting, better gather up all the gear. Winter won't approve of his tools rusting out in the woods. We'll take it back to the cottage. You and Tom can manage that while we take the stretcher."

Arthur, meanwhile, had lost consciousness again, but he revived when the doctor appeared. A quick examination proved that there was no internal injury. Arthur had escaped death by an inch or two. He was given an injection, and after a few moments he was lifted gently onto the stretcher, and Sir George, with the three men, followed by the doctor and the boys laden with the tools, formed a slow procession through the woods to the cottage.

Mrs. Winter showed her true character. Her anxieties vanished. She and Margaret had the bedroom ready, and she came out to the stretcher. "Why, Arthur, what you up to now?" She leaned over him, speaking so gently that Margaret turned aside, for the first time overcome, after facing the accident so bravely and practically.

"I can't let you out of my sight," said Mrs. Winter. "And you, Tom! You go and see those tools are put away as he like 'em to be. You know how particular he is!"

An hour later the doctor left. The broken arm was set, and Arthur quiet under the drug, his face cleaned up and bandaged.

The Squire and his men went off, leaving Billy with Tom.

"Well, that's it," said Billy. "Margaret put up a good show, didn't she?"

Tom was still shaken, but the job of putting the tools away in the shed, with Billy's help, had calmed him down. They stood at the door now, Billy preparing to follow his father home to lunch.

"Where is she now?" asked Tom.

"She was upstairs with your mother. I bet she was glad of the help. Women are like that."

"So are men, aren't they?" said Tom, stupidly.

He was unable to think clearly, but deep down inside he was rejoicing. Billy had stood by him, and so had Margaret. It was good to have friends. He told himself that, but he said nothing about it to Billy, who quietly walked around to the front of the cottage and up the lane. Tom watched him for a while and saw Billy turn, put his fingers to his mouth, and give a long whistle, a cheerful sound.

12 Salt in the Wound

Arthur Winter was in bed for a week, and when he got up, he could only sit about indoors, his right arm in plaster. He was very grumpy and, like most strong people when sick, made a great fuss.

"How do I know I ain't done for?" was his repeated cry. "Squire won't want my service if I can't swing an ax."

"Such rubbish as you talk!" retorted Mrs. Winter during one of these lamentations when her husband was really much better and all the more irritable about not being able to use his arm. "Should be thankful you're alive, man. Might have been in your grave by now, and me left here with Tom. A nice thing that would have been."

But her care for him was kinder than her words. Lady Lander had sent a small barrel of beer to the cottage, among other gifts of fuel and things for the larder. To see Mrs. Winter drawing a glass of ale for her disabled man, studying the froth on it, putting it gently down beside

him, and then filling his pipe with tobacco brought from the Hall by Billy was a lesson in gentleness and devotion.

For the rest of the school holidays, however, Tom had to be the man about the house, and the only meetings with his friend were when Billy called at the cottage, usually with a full basket sent from the Hall.

He was not the only visitor. Fellow workers on the estate and their wives rallied helpfully around Mrs. Winter and Tom. The only regular one was Margaret Sims, who

came every day and insisted on helping with the house-
work, a kindness which embarrassed Mrs. Winter, who
was particular, as she said to Tom, about being under an
obligation to nobody.

"Would have been nice if we'd had a girl like that,"
said Arthur to his wife one afternoon, when sitting down
to a tea table which Margaret had laid before leaving
early to avoid a walk home in the dark. "Would have
been company for our Tom, to have had a sister."

"The sooner you get back to your work, the better,"
said Mrs. Winter. And Tom, who overheard this conversation between his parents, thought so too. Now that his
father was on the road to recovery, Tom began to be
bored with having to hang around the cottage, at beck
and call of these two disturbed grown-ups, though he had
been anxious enough and sympathetic enough all through
the crisis and the days when his help was needed.

He missed the freedom of his outdoor life, the closeness
to all that went on, day and night, in the forest, and along
the coast, and through the open country between. And
he had begun to notice that Billy's visits were growing
shorter and more infrequent.

"You don't need to come down here if you don't want
to," he said one day when Billy called in only an hour
before nightfall. It was again the last day of the holidays.

"Why d'you say that, Tom?"

Tom knew well enough, but he did not want to confess.
"I don't know," he said. But it was not the truth. Even
so, he might have spoken up and regretted it, had not the
cause of his trouble unexpectedly appeared.

"I've been sent to fetch my sister," said Harold Sims as
Tom opened the door. "She ought to be home before
dark."

This was the first time Tom had seen him since the adventure on the seashore on the day after the Christmas party at the Hall.

"She might be living here," Harold continued. He did not enter, but he saw Billy standing in front of the kitchen stove that looked so small in the great blocked-up fireplace.

"Oh, you here, Billy?" he cried familiarly. "Visiting the tenantry?"

A surge of anger blinded Tom Winter. It seemed that he could not meet Harold Sims without losing control of his normally quiet temper.

At that moment Mrs. Winter came in from the scullery, where she was cutting her husband's hair. "Your sister went home an hour ago, young man," she said severely. Her humility did not extend to newly rich towns-people who intruded into country life.

"Oh, thanks," said Harold. He hesitated, then spoke over Tom's still angry body. "You coming along, Billy? We'll go back together."

Billy was uncomfortable. He had only just arrived, to set down his basket on the table and to spend an hour with Tom on this last day of the Christmas holidays. But during Tom's unavoidable extra duties at home owing to his father's accident, Billy had accepted Harold's approaches, for the boy was lonely enough as a newcomer to the neighborhood. They had been about together, and Billy had even got permission from Sir George to take this newcomer out with their guns, to initiate him into the art of rough shooting, and to cure him of taking an excited potshot at every moving object in sight.

Billy had not thought it advisable to tell Tom Winter

95

about these adventures. He was something of a politician but had no thought of disloyalty to his lifetime friend. Furher, the was rather bored with Sims's clumsiness with a gun, the futile efforts to train the Airedale, and the equally obvious efforts to ingratiate himself with the Squire's son. Such things were not worth mentioning to Tom Winter, who in Billy's opinion would not understand so complicated a matter.

Billy was not prepared for Tom's overquiet intuition and sensitiveness, which showed themselves in the form of downright jealousy, a passion which now spoke out.

Tom stepped back from the doorway, to allow free passage. "That's right," he said bitterly. "You'd better go back together."

Billy looked at him in dismay, which turned to anger. "Oh, if that's how you feel, I will." And he walked out to join Harold Sims, who could not resist a triumphant parting shot, a practice he was good at.

He said, over his shoulder, "Sorry to hear about your father. Pretty clumsy of him to get knocked down like that."

That was the end of the Christmas holidays, the time of goodwill to all men.

13 New Life

The winter term was hard for Tom. His father rested at home, almost helpless, for a month, while the broken arm was mending. Arthur, an active and independent man, turned irritable in idleness, and this tried Mrs. Winter's patience. There was little peace in the woodman's cottage.

Tom could not escape because he had to do the man's jobs about the house and garden. He chopped the firewood, carried the coal, cleared the snow from the paths after every fall—a hundred and one jobs that kept him busy before and after school.

But that was not the cause of his misery. He was unhappy because he was hurt and humiliated. Something had come into his life which he had never known before, something evil and threatening. He could not understand what it was, but it centered itself in the person of the newcomer, Harold Sims, whose contempt and dislike bewildered him.

Added to that was the still more bewildering conduct of Billy Lander. Since that parting in anger at the end of the Christmas holidays, there had been no message from Billy. Last term he had sent a postcard, but now, nothing.

Tom, in his loneliness and winter gloom, magnified

Billy's silence and saw it as an end to their friendship.

He had no other friends, this woodland boy. Billy was part of his life.

So the winter days passed, with darkness hardly lifted from the silent, empty world when Tom left the cottage in the morning and darkness falling again by the time he got home from school.

After the beginning of February the long frost broke, and wind and rain scoured the earth. Silence and snow vanished together. Now it was "water, water everywhere," overflowing the ditches, carrying mud out to sea, seeping under loose tiles, flooding lowlying meadows, bringing down frost-loosened sections of the cliffs.

The days began to lengthen, but Tom did not take advantage of the spells of daylight because he was still too unhappy to resume his old habit of rambling in the forest and along the sea-shore, taking part in the wildlife and the rest of the outdoor drama. He had lost the faculty of curiosity. Tom Winter was sorry for himself.

One Saturday afternoon, when Tom was moping about indoors, though the rough weather had given way to pale sunshine, Arthur came in from his workshop.

" 'Tisn't no use," he said. "Can't do a job with one hand. But I've been a burden, Tom, I've been a burden. It's not like me to put your mother into a temper. I reckon it's time I looked around a bit and got out from under her feet."

Tom looked at his father in astonishment, and saw the cheerful easygoing person he had known all his life before the accident.

"You've got a load on your shoulders, boy. What's come over you these days? Why don't we take a walk together? Seems as though we want a shake-up in this place. Mother gone shopping, hasn't she? We'll set off to meet her and carry her basket."

Tom agreed, but listlessly. Nothing interested him. He might as well be out-of-doors as in.

No sooner were they in the open than Arthur changed his mind. He sniffed the moist, warm air and stared up at the sun, his face alight with pleasure. He drew a deep breath.

"Ah!" he exclaimed. "That be good, Tom! There's a change about. 'Tis what we want. I reckon I smell a touch of spring. We been that down this winter, since I took that knock. Upset us all, it seems. You ain't yourself, boy, and Mother fretting for fear I lose my job. But Sir George is a good master. Paid my wages regular every week. 'Tisn't all who are that lucky, I fancy."

Then he drank another great draft of the fresh air, which inspired him to say, "Nay, Tom! We'll walk through the forest. 'Tis many a day since I went up by the inner rides. The moor out beyond will be good on a day like this. 'Tis time enough, and a moon to guide us home if we pass nightfall."

Even disconsolate Tom caught something of Arthur's enthusiasm, and father and son set off along the familiar ride that led through the forest from the gate in the garden behind the cottage.

The change of weather had encouraged other creatures, as well as Arthur Winter. From a treetop near the edge of the woods a mistle thrush was shouting his challenge to the universe at large, repeating each variation of it three times, just to make sure there was no mistake.

"That old bird do go it!" said Arthur. "He don't care what may happen; another freeze-up or no!"

99

Certainly the song set all the forest responding. The wind blew, the trees swayed, branches squeaked against branches, and topmost twigs flicked out like whips, though down below all was comparatively quiet.

"There he goes, Dad, there he goes!" cried Tom, suddenly waking out of his indifference.

He pointed to a fox far ahead. The red-flanked creature slunk across the ride, head down in front and tail down behind, sniffing after something unseen. Sensing the approach of human beings, it turned its head and glowered at them, and then went on, indifferent, but perhaps a little faster.

"Up to no good, I'll lay," said Arthur.

"But he's a beauty, Dad."

"You don't be particular, Tom, eh? Proper lover you are, of all things in the open. Never knew such a lad. Well, it don't do you no discredit, I'd say. Feel that way myself maybe. But I've more an eye for the stewpot! Needs must, I suppose. But I bears no grudge to any beast, be it stoat or other vermin. They've got to live, like the rest of us. We all have to take our chance, though."

With that wise remark to end a long speech, Arthur Winter chuckled, from the sheer pleasure of being alive and on the way back to his usual good health and freedom of movement. He could now use his right arm in a rough-and-ready sort of way, though the plaster still held it stiff. This rigid coating was by now nicely colored down, like a piece of antique statuary. It no longer prevented Arthur from fumbling for his tobacco tin and filling his pipe. Tom waited patiently while his father lighted up and puffed a preliminary cloud of fragrant smoke that was at once seized and thinned away horizontally between the tree trunks and tangle of hanging bramble, old-man's-beard, and the rest of the withered skeletons of last summer's undergrowth.

"Good to be warm, Tom!" said Arthur, stepping off with his son again; and he put his free arm along Tom's shoulder. "How much longer are they going to keep you at schooling, lad?"

Tom knew what was coming next.

"Time you took a hand along with me, I reckon. A lot to learn in woodcraft, though I don't say you ain't shaping well."

Tom felt a glow of new life. He knew his father's good-hearted simplicity and revered his craftsmanship, which he was already beginning to share. But he was also his mother's son, and that was a very different matter.

"There's a lot to learn nowadays, Dad."

"What, all that bookwork? That don't teach you the way of the woods and the nature of the trees, every kind and degree. They be as various in they little ways as us folk, Tom. You have to know about that. Yes, and all that lives in them and moves about under them. That's one thing I'll say for Squire. He knows these things, and he knows I know. That be the reason he puts up with my little ways."

"What little ways?"

Tom need not ask that question, but he could not resist teasing his father, just as his mother could not resist warning him, even while she stirred the replenished stewpot.

"You young rascal," said Arthur, giving Tom a hug as they walked on deeper into the forest, down a dip that gave to a tiny brook on its way through the woods westward, to join the stream which over the last million or more years had carved out the valley overlooked by the

Hall and lower down by the White Elephant, the stream that widened beyond the village, to the estuary and the sea.

They dropped into the dip in the forest and crossed the stream by a plank bridge. The water was up, almost submerging the two planks, swirling thick with mud. A few patches of ice lingered along its banks, for the cold still clung in that hollow—a dark area, where the sunlight hardly ever penetrated, even in high summer. Skeletons of ferns and sedge grass wavered and trembled in the flow of the high water.

"I reckon this be always a solemn spot," said Arthur. "All manner of life hiding about here."

As though to prove this, a movement downstream drew their attention. A large animal moved out of cover onto a flat stretch where the brook widened, now almost overflowing the pebbly bed that normally formed a tiny island.

"Look, Dad!" cried Tom. "It's a badger."

"So it be, Tom. You've got quick sight, boy. That's right. See his head; there's the black stripes and the white. Proper old clown, he looks! Minds his own business, he does."

They stood watching him, as he paused midstream, snuffling about like a rooting pig, then landing on the right-hand bank, where he lingered until suddenly he spotted the two spectators, when he lumbered off downstream and disappeared.

"When I was a boy, folks used to bait them with dogs. Used to box them up in a hole, chained by the tail, and let the dogs in. But Old Brock would give a good account of himself before he was killed. He'd often finish off two or three dogs before he was done."

He was about to add more to his story but stopped, because Tom was shivering and staring blankly into space, as at a ghost.

"What's up, boy?" said Arthur sharply. "You taken sick like?"

Tom shook his head, to bring himself back to earth.

"No! But I don't like that idea—it's evil. It's like that boy Sims setting his dog on to the hare."

And he told his father the story.

Arthur studied him sidelong, puffing thoughtfully at his pipe.

"You got to live in this world, Tom, my lad. It don't do to take on too much. You'll make a peck of trouble for yourself that way. There's more of his kind than of yours, I'd say. 'Tis the way nature works, too!"

Arthur moved on, and Tom with him, but not without a glance or two backward in the hope of catching sight of the badger again.

After a period of silence, while they left the dip and rose to the other side where the forest began to thin out toward the open moorland, northward, Tom belatedly commented on his father's last words. "But it's not all cruel, Dad. I've seen gentle things done."

Arthur agreed, and they gave each other examples of the care and devotion shown by feather and fur, especially in the mating and breeding seasons, the seasons of display and of song, of building and feeding, rather than of combat. Arthur had to bring Tom down, or around, to reality again.

"But they've got to live and to feed their young. That means hunting, Tom, which ain't a pretty business."

The afternoon was closing down, and already the sunlight was filtering through the purple mists over the horizon. They came to still more open ground, where the forest had been thinned years before, and sweet chestnut, now bare, had put up new growth. Arthur decided upon the return home.

They sat for a while, to rest on a tree stump.

"I cut that soon after you were born." Arthur cleared the damp moss off the flat surface, disturbing a variety of small creatures: spiders, wood lice, which scuttled away from their snug winter retreat.

"Time we replanted some oak, Tom. 'Tis a shame to take and not restore. See how them chestnuts and those birch are crowding up. But it's oak we want for the future. I'd better talk to Mr. Hogg about that. He'll put Squire on to it sharp enough. A great man for oak, Mr. Hogg. He never did like working in beech, but I daren't say so to Sir George, for all his masterful ways."

Tom listened to this professional soliloquy, while engaged more consciously in looking around him. The friendly walk with his father had cheered him, restored his confidence. He was alert again and ready for the sight which now caught his attention.

Out where the thinning trees ended in open moorland, the late afternoon light picked up every detail, as though heather, gorse bushes, elder and hawthorn were lighted up from within, burning with a cold, unconsuming fire, almost brighter than the northern sky above the scene. This reversal of light between earth and sky made illusion possible. Dusk already gathered in the air.

For a moment, therefore, Tom hardly noticed that something was approaching over the moor. It might have been a handsbreadth of mist, rising from a dewpond. It was a mere shadow. But it grew more substantial and took a definite shape, coming nearer.

"Dad!" whispered Tom. "See it?"

He felt the blood flushing over his face and a tingling sensation under his cap. He dreaded making any movement, and his hands pressed palm downward on the tree stump where he sat. His whole attention, mind, body, concentrated, and for those few first moments of recognition, nothing else in the universe existed.

The shape proved to be two objects, forming out of the open landscape, coming forward against the setting sun to be defined by it: the dappled gray doe and, close to her flank, an almost pure white fawn. They moved demurely, but full of trust, nearer to the two human beings, not yet seeing this intrusion into their world. The fawn was playful, but shy, for it pressed against its mother's side, causing her to turn her head, as though reproving it, and to edge a little sideways, so that their progress was like that of a yacht tacking, for when the fawn was left, it gave a tiny leap, like a step in a dance, and the doe moved back to it again, protectively.

So this casual progress brought them nearer. Neither Tom nor his father said a word. They watched and waited on this almost unearthly spectacle, this sudden appearance of two creatures out of fairyland. The waning light added to the unreality. It seemed to make them transparent, of no weight, with the lifeblood observable, coursing in their veins.

Then suddenly the scent of tobacco smoke, drifting from Arthur's pipe, reached the mother's nostrils. She stopped. She lifted her head, sniffing at the air, moving her head from right to left, left to right. She was clearly puzzled, suspicious.

Nothing happened for a moment; then she saw the two figures on the tree stump, though they must have been almost invisible against the dark background of trees with the recesses of the forest beyond.

Instantly she turned, put herself between this likely danger and her fawn, nosing it round, nudging it. The little white phantom thereupon followed suit, turning as its mother directed and galloping after her as she trotted away, first slowly, then gathering speed as her fear goaded her on.

Soon she merged into the many shapes over the moorland, from which the light was rapidly fading. Last to be seen was the little white fawn, leaping over the tummocks, joyous in its chase of the mother, whose dappled sides were no longer visible.

Tom sat there, still flushed, with his hands pressed down on the tree stump. "I saw them, Dad," he said, with a break in his voice, as though he had been crying, But he was exultant. "I saw them," he repeated.

Arthur knocked out his pipe. "Aye," he said. "That be the first—and a white one, too. Don't often see the like o' that in nature. But it happens. I've seen a white squirrel and a white hare. They usually have pink eyes and don't fare decently. Too conspicuous, I suppose. And 'tis said they don't have normal eyesight, which goes against them in the fight for life. No, they be freaks and stand no chance."

Then he noticed that Tom appeared to be in a trance. "Come, lad," he said sharply. "Your mother will be home first and fretting about us."

Tom got up and walked after his father in silence.

14 A Letter from Billy

The next day was Sunday, and Arthur invited Tom to go with him to the Hall before Sir George and Lady Lander went to church. He must report the birth of the white fawn, as a memorable event.

They duly presented themselves at ten o'clock before the kitchen door in the courtyard of the Hall. Lady Lander was in the kitchen talking to the cook.

"Why, Winter!" she said. "And how is the arm? Looks as though that grubby old plaster should come off. What does the doctor think? I tell you, we all had a fright. Margaret Sims has written regularly from school; she can't forget it. A nice child, that. Rather lonely, I think.

"And you, Tom," she cried. "You've not been in all this term. Why, you've changed in appearance! You look a year older, quite elderly and solemn. What's got into you, Tom?"

Cook, meanwhile, poured two cups of tea from a huge pot which stood permanently in service under a cozy on the long kitchen table.

"Aye, m'lady. Tom's been that way since what we saw yesterday up on the moor," said Arthur Winter, much to Tom's embarrassment.

"Why, whatever do you mean?" said Lady Lander
sharply. But she put her arm around Tom's shoulders
with such warm kindliness that he spilled some tea into
the saucer and thus added to his discomfort, for he knew
that his mother would be shocked if he poured the tea
from his saucer back into the cup. But Lady Lander did
it for him, while she listened to Arthur's tale of the
apparition of the gray doe and the white fawn.

"Why, bless their hearts, but how lovely!" she cried.
"Do you hear that, Cook: a white doe? It was another
doe, was it not, Winter?"

"We couldn't rightly tell, m'lady. 'Twas coming over
dark when we met them, and they was off like a couple
of ghosts, as you might say."

"It is marvelous, Winter. How right of you to come
up to tell us! This must be the first of the season—rather
early. Sir George will be delighted."

"Billy ought to know," said Tom eagerly.

"Yes. Why don't you write and tell him, Tom? Have you written this term?"

"No. Nor has he."

Tom was guarded, and Lady Lander looked at him in surprise. "Why, nothing wrong, is there?"

Tom did not answer, but his troubled face and the change in his manner, which Lady Lander had remarked earlier, set her thinking. The lifelong friendship between the two boys had been the talk of the countryside. "You've got the address of the school, have you not?" she said.

Tom nodded. He could not trust himself to speak. Bitterness still lay like the dregs of poison in his mind.

"Well, what's to stop your writing to him? I expect he's wondering why you haven't. But boys are like that. We only hear from Billy when he wants something. Not like Margaret Sims. I should think we've had three or four letters from her this term. She might be one of the family. I wonder if she writes home as often. It's a step-mother, isn't it?"

She did not wait for replies to her broadside of questions but left the kitchen and could be heard in the front of the Hall, calling Sir George, to return with him.

"Well, Winter! What's this? A freak in the herd? But how charming. A white doe! We'll put it on the family crest, my love."

Sir George turned from his wife to talk more seriously to Arthur. "So you were up at the moor? I've been thinking about that. How long since we cleared the trees there?"

"It would be when both the boys were down with

measles," said Arthur solemnly. "That's nigh on ten years ago. They'd be about three years old, I'd say."

"Can't believe it, Winter. Heavens! The way time slips along; faster every year. This estate is too much for me. Always discovering something we've neglected. I'll speak to Hogg, and we'll go up there and decide what to do."

"I know what he wants to do, sir. They was oak trees we felled, and oak trees it should be again."

"Good heavens! That's a long-term policy, Winter. But you are right. I can't bear these plantations of spruce which are springing up all over the country for the sake of quick money."

"Well, that be forty year," said Arthur.

"Yes, but not four hundred, Winter, you rogue!" Then the Squire became more personal. "What about that arm? We can't do much until you're whole again."

"I'd like to say thank you, sir, in respect of that."

"Nonsense, man," said Sir George gruffly. "We're one big family on this estate, I hope. The thing is to keep going in our own old-fashioned way, if only they will let us."

Tom wondered what Sir George meant by "they" and found himself picturing Harold Sims's father and the group of men with whom he had been talking at the Christmas party.

"Well, Tom, you're the naturalist on the estate. What do you think of this latest addition to our stock?"

Tom had drunk his tea, so now there was no danger of spilling it. But the compliment of being called a naturalist, even though it was true, caused him to blush with pleasure.

"It's...it's a miracle!" he stammered, so intense was he,

so full of feelings he could not express, that his eagerness caused Sir George to clap him on the shoulder and Lady Lander to cry out: "Don't dislocate the boy, darling! And you, Tom, see that you write and tell Billy, or he'll never forgive you. Such a thing as this! It's never happened before, has it, George?"

Tom thought over this advice for the rest of the day, and on Monday it haunted him during school hours. But he did not write his letter on Monday night. He wanted to, but something held him back.

That is why Billy got in first. There was a letter from him. The postman brought it on Tuesday morning. A letter at the woodman's cottage was such a rare thing that the postman was offered a cup of tea from the breakfast pot, and he got to talking.

"Seems these new people up at the big house are settling down to our country life," he said to Arthur, who sat by the stove while Mrs. Winter fastened his gaiters after lacing up his boots, he meanwhile enjoying a pipe. He was going down to the doctor's surgery in the village, to see about getting his arm released from that plaster. This information was imparted to the postman, whose remark about the Sims family was meanwhile overlooked.

"Aye," said the postman. "It hasn't seemed natural like, not seeing you about in the woods, though I have no occasion to go up there during my round. But I take a stroll there once in a while; postman's holiday, I call it. Last time I was up there, I saw that youngster from the big house. Stalking round, he was, with a twelve-bore gun as big as himself. Reckon he must have borrowed it unbeknown to his dad."

"Old Peter Apps will have a word to say to him, if he lights on him," said Arthur Winter. "He's respect of nobody where his game is concerned—not even his work-mates."

Arthur chuckled, over old memories, and certain friendly understanding.

"That's what I says," added the postman. "When I saw the boy, I thought to myself that these townsfolk take things up a bit too quick, like our country ways."

Tom listened to all this in silence. Any reminder of Harold Sims made him feel uncomfortable, uneasy. He was eager to read Billy's letter. He knew it was from Billy, for nobody else in the world would write to him. So he retreated to the kitchen and the light through the back window over the sink, to read the letter against the accompaniment of conversation from the front room.

DEAR TOM (said Billy's letter), Second term nearly over. Looking forward to Easter holidays and shall be glad to see you. Not so good here this term, though one has to be civil all around. One or two rotters who make it difficult to be civil. Some people don't understand our ways. Keep a lookout for me. I'll be down to the cottage as soon as you like. Any news of the Sims family? That girl is good value, best of the bunch. She must join us sometimes. Home soon.

Yours,
BILLY

Tom read the letter twice. It was like listening to Billy. It smoothed things out. He put it in his pocket, and all day at school it warmed him. He learned more from it than he did from the blackboard.

That evening he wrote to Billy and told him about the doe and the white fawn. He had so much to say about

113

this that the letter was long and eloquent. He forgot to mention the Sims family or to refer to Billy's remark about Margaret. Or he may not have forgotten. That uneasiness at the back of his mind may have prevented him.

He posted the letter on the way to school next day. Billy's letter was still in his pocket, part of his private possessions. It made him feel more sure of himself, as he always felt when he was with Billy.

15 The Return of Spring

As the days lengthened and life showed signs
of returning to the moorland and forest, everywhere on
land even down to the sea's edge, Arthur Winter ventured more and more, by the sheer force of his healthy
body and his simple, concentrated willpower, strengthen-
ing the arm, now free of the plaster of Paris which had
protected it for two months.

Tom's broken pride was not so easily healed. Even that
letter from Billy had not put things right. But there was
something else, not easily to be explained. It was something which drove him out every day, whenever he could
snatch an hour from jobs at home, out of school hours.
Off he went, wandering in the forest, usually up to the
moor where he had first seen the vision on that Saturday
afternoon at the end of winter.

He had always been eager to share the life of the woodlands, the moors, meadows, and the sea. Bird, beast, ant
and beetle were part of his family, necessary to him, day
by day. But this other thing, the apparition of the doe
with her white fawn, was an overwhelming experience.
It filled him with an excitement that set him longing for
he knew not what. It haunted him, and he could not rest
until he found the fabulous little creature again.

But the days, the weeks passed, and he had no luck. He ranged the woods and frequently encountered the herd of fallow deer or groups of them, but the doe and her fawn were never to be numbered there. Perhaps they had been rejected because of the whiteness of the fawn. Tom wondered about this. It worried him. He felt it was something to do with his own life, so solitary now that Billy had gone away to school and changed the pattern of things.

"What ails you, boy?" said Mrs. Winter to Tom one morning when he came in to breakfast after tiring himself walking, seeking vainly in the paths for a sight of the fawn, puzzling his brains over the mystery of its never being there, of its invisibility.

"I can't find it," he said, and he was so weary after the search, so hungry and disappointed, that he burst into tears.

This made his mother very cross.

"Such nonsense!" she cried. It was her usual response to things beyond her comprehension. "Can't find what? Whatever is the matter with you? Why, you're getting as thin as a lath. First, it's your father, and now it's you worrying me. All these notions in your head, as though there isn't enough in the world to think of."

Tom quickly pulled himself together, helped by a plate of hot porridge and a mug of tea, with several slices of brown bread and honey. He listened to his mother almost blissfully, comforted by her homely grumble, because it was so familiar. He took it naturally, as it came, just as he took the changes of the weather.

"I don't believe you've heard a word," cried Mrs. Winter. "Sitting there with that look on your face. I sometimes think that you're beside yourself, dreaming the days away like a little gentleman. I know what it is. It's that keeping company with Master William ever since you both could run about together. I don't think milady should have allowed it. But the boy sought you out, and that's honestly said! I knew it would come to this. Now he's had to go off into his own world and leave you in yours. And I tell you, my son, they are different worlds, as I've said all along."

Arthur came down to breakfast.

"What's all this, Mother?" he said. "Leave the boy be, at this time of day. You worry at things like a terrier. What's he done wrong? You should be thankful he's a quiet enough lad. You might have had a whelp like that sour little—"

"Now don't *you* add to it," cried Mrs. Winter. "It's enough to have him in the morning like a ghost rather than a healthy child," and it was her turn to burst into tears, to the utter astonishment of her good husband.

"Nay, Mother," he said. "I better be given my breakfast. I be going to make a start at some sort of a day's work. Devil knows how handy I'll be with my tools after all these months. But I'll put my hands to them, and be damned to all this fancy stuff and woman's notions. So put a stop to it!"

And she did. Still with the tears in her eyes and on her cheeks, she ladled out a plate of porridge and quite humbly put it down before her man, who grunted and began to eat.

Tom, meanwhile, searched for his satchel, put his face up to his mother's wet cheek, said something unintelligible to his father, and left for school.

The March morning was wild, but warm. A high wind, sweeping in gusty blasts, drove great pillows of cloud across the sky at speed, so that the sunshine spun round and about like the beams from a lighthouse. Everything seemed to be on the move. The woods groaned in their roots, almost torn out of the ground, tossing in violent protest. Clouds of last year's leaves blew out from the edges of the forest, like flights of maddened sparrows. Rooks and starlings, in the sky, outstripped by the clouds, appeared to be flying backward and sideways, demented with the rest of nature.

Tom leaned against the crazy weather, glad of the struggle. He felt the air filling his lungs, filling them over-full and making him drunk. He wanted to shout, but his voice would not be heard amid this universal commotion. No matter: nothing mattered. He was released. He felt good. Something had happened during breakfast, something deeper than tears and his mother's grumbling.

Easter was on its way, and the world was waking up. Soon the holidays would begin, with Billy home again.

Tom strode on against the southwester, his satchel bumping against his back as the wind got under and lifted it. The surface of the lane glittered, swept clean of dust and debris. He reached the junction and the gateway to the drive into the big house, the White Elephant, as Lady Lander had christened it.

There at the gate stood Margaret Sims.

"Why aren't you at school?" said Tom, but the wind caught his words and twisted them up like a spiral of smoke. Margaret, however, had anticipated his question.

"We've broken up early, with an outbreak of mumps. I got home yesterday and thought I might see you on your way to school. The others won't be home for nearly a week."

Tom knew whom she meant, and for the first time on this joyous morning he was reminded of Harold Sims. But even that could not dampen his revival of good spirits.

"I had a letter from Billy," he said. "And he mentioned you in it."

Margaret tossed back the hair windblown across her face. And then she laughed.

"Oh, Billy!" she said. "He's everybody's friend. Not like you, Tom. You're difficult."

"What do you mean?" said Tom. "I've done you no harm."

She laughed again. "You idiot! Now I'll walk a little way with you. I've nothing else to do."

They had not gone far along the road to the village

when Margaret spoke again. "What's this news about a freak among the herd of deer? Will Sir George keep it, this white oddity? I wish he'd let me have it. I'd love it as a pet."

Tom shrank away from her. She had taken his arm while asking about the deer.

"That wouldn't do," he said huskily, and he quickened his pace.

"There, you see!" said Margaret at this rebuff. "There's nothing of Billy in you. You're always ready to be hurt. What have I said now? D'you think I don't understand, Tom?"

"Sorry," he answered. They walked on without talking for a while, and the world rocked more wildly about them as they approached the village and the sea. "But this is different. You couldn't make a pet of it. It's something different."

He could not explain further, and Margaret did not attempt to make him do so.

"I won't come any farther," she said. They stood for a moment. "But you'll let me see it, won't you, Tom?"

Tom hesitated. "I've only seen it once," he said. "I've been looking for it every day since. That's weeks ago—but no sign. My dad was with me; so we both saw it."

"It wasn't one of your dreams then," said Margaret. "Oh, Tom, you're so odd!"

She turned and walked away, and the wind followed her, blowing her hair over her head and face. Tom heard her laughter as she struggled against the elements.

Then he walked on, puzzled by what she had said.

16 A Consultation

Easter came, and with it a spell of good weather after the March winds. It also brought Billy Lander and Harold Sims home from school.

Billy was as good as his word in the short letter written to Tom during term time. He came down to the cottage the day after he got home and brought a message from the Squire for Arthur Winter.

He found only Mrs. Winter, who was making the most of the fine weather by washing the winter blankets.

"Tom's at school, Master William," she said, wiping her wet arms, "and my man's up in the woods some-where. He reckons to use that arm again, but I'm uneasy over those heavy axes. They give a good jolt to a weak limb."

"Not with his skill, Mrs. Winter," said Billy. "I've seen him at work. He makes it as gentle as you like. He might be cutting a cheese!"

"Ah, you're too easy, Master William."

"No, I'm one of the family. That's my father's creed, Mrs. Winter, and it's in my blood. We all belong here."

"So that's why you be so friendly with my Tom?"

Billy studied Mrs. Winter before he replied. "I've never thought of it," he said. "We were born together; I suppose that's how it is—and both born here."

This must have been so conclusive that it brought Arthur Winter back into the cottage. "Why, young William," he said, and Mrs. Winter winced at the familiarity. "You home from school already? Tom is still at his lessons. He'll be a more learned man than you if you don't watch it!"

"He's that already," was the smooth retort. "At least in the things that matter, most of which he's learned from you, Arthur."

Arthur took this good-naturedly. Praise or blame passed over his head. He was assured in his craftsmanship, and better than some. That was his creed.

"My father wants you to meet him and Mr. Hogg up at the big clearing by the moor," said Billy. "I'd like to come with you. We may see this fawn that Tom told me about in his letter."

"Aye, he did that? Pretty little creature it was, too fair for this world, I reckon," said Arthur. "Tom has been searching for it every day since we saw it with the gray doe coming across the moor. A good sight it was, the pair of them trotting toward us where we sat quiet like. If I'd not been smoking my pipe, they'd have come right up to us. But the doe caught that whiff of my tobacco, and off they went like shadows. Put young Tom into a proper trance, that did."

"Yes, his letter was full of it. It's as though he is frightened."

Arthur did not like that. "Tom ain't a boy to be frightened," he said. "Leastways, nothing in nature would scare him. Why's he's out day and night on his own. No, it's his mother's place to be frightened, and on his behalf."

" 'Tis not what he does, but what he is that sometimes puts me about," said Mrs. Winter. "Going around with his head full of dreams."

"Nay, Mother, there's nothing wrong with the lad. What say you, William?"

But Billy was not to be drawn into a family argument.

"Well," he said, "shall we go? I was to tell you that you were to meet them this morning about eleven. It's a good walk through the forest, so we should set off."

"I'll take me little notebook," said Arthur. "With Mr. Hogg about there is bound to be more orders than a man can remember."

Arthur moved a tea chest on the beam above the fireplace and took down a greasy black notebook, secured with a rubber band, which also retained a stub of pencil.

"Looks as though they be thinking of replanting up there. If that be so, I takes my stand on oak. Oak it was, and oak it should be again."

With that determination, he and Billy set off, leaving Mrs. Winter to her washtub. They talked of this and that on their way along the ride that rose gradually toward the moor.

"See those primroses through there," said Arthur, pointing to a dip where several elder bushes were draped with long strands of honeysuckle already green with new life.

"Yes," said Billy. "Pity Tom isn't here. He'd like to see that."

Winter looked down at him with amusement. "Oh! You and Tom! A proper pair, I'd say. What's to come of it, Master William?"

Billy was startled by Arthur's formality. "Why, what d'you mean?" he said.

"Only this: your ways will be different later on. I reckon on that boy taking my place as woodman when I am gone. Then you will be master and man. How about that, young sir?"

Billy pondered for some moments as they walked on, he in front.

"If ever that makes any difference," he said at last, "it will be Tom's doing, not mine. He's the one who is touchy. Look how he's taken against Sims, hardly ever civil to him, and resents it because I am."

Then he laughed. "Not that I blame him. But Sims lives here now, and we can't shut him out."

"No, you won't shut him out," said Arthur dryly. "Proper young hunter, he'll be, by all accounts, with his gun and his dog."

"What? He's got a gun?"

"I'll say no more. I've no cause to favor that lad, and I'd better not speak."

This might have caused an embarrassing silence between them, had they not reached a junction of rides and been joined by the gamekeeper, old Peter Apps, who approached from westward.

"We be summoned then?" he said, after greeting Billy and Arthur, shifting his gun from one arm to the other,

124

and ordering his sheep dog to be less friendly to the young master, who had a magnetic attraction for all dogs, which drew them to him, slavering with affection.

"Down boy. Get behind there! Down, Rover!"

Rover obeyed. He got behind, but behind Billy, nudging up to him with a wet nose from time to time, to be reprimanded by a growl from his master.

So they proceeded, rising through the forest toward the moor, when suddenly Rover stiffened, stopped and was nearly trodden on by Arthur. Rover began to pace forward, slowly, deliberately, growling in a sort of dangerous undertone.

"Ut yer," said Apps. "Ut yer."

But Rover was not to be subdued. A moment later the cause was discovered. Harold Sims's Airedale was quartering the woods. It leaped out into the ride, and sprang at Rover. A savage battle began, with the clumsy young Airedale at first all over the sheep dog. But Rover, mature and cunning, quickly recovered and was about to teach his assailant a lesson, had he not been drawn off by his master, while Billy seized the Airedale by the collar and pulled him aside. Both dogs were electric with fury and were still being held apart when Harold Sims appeared. He had been beating his way under the trees and was carrying a gun.

"Sorry about that," he said to Billy. "Is it your dog? I'm afraid mine is pretty fierce. It's the breed."

"No, it isn't my dog," said Billy.

"Oh," said Sims, changing his tune. He turned to the gamekeeper, who still held Rover back. "You should keep your dog under control," said Sims.

Peter Apps's response was to release Rover and to say something quietly to him. The dog sat on his haunches,

125

looking up at Peter for further orders. The old man turned to the boy.

"You be new here, young feller, eh? Have you got a license for that gun? And have you got permission from the Squire to cover these woods? I think I'd have heard of it if you had. Seems you were seen last Christmas holidays with that gun. But now I see for myself. Let me warn you, young man. You're not of an age yet to have that freedom. A twelve-bore gun is a man's weapon. Perhaps your dad may know something about it, or he may not, if you have borrowed it unbeknown, eh? Is that it?"

Harold Sims was red-faced, but with rage, not shame. He turned on Arthur Winter. "That's your doing, I expect," he said. "Who else would have been interested in my affairs?"

Arthur was so amazed that he stood helpless and left the matter to Peter Apps, who had not moved for fear that Rover might have taken a movement as a signal of release, for a renewed attack on the stranger in his domain.

The old man was quite calm. He looked at Harold Sims almost mildly as he spoke. "That's an old head on young shoulders you've got, young master. But it's not a wise one. You be come from town. You've got a lot to learn of our country ways, and that can be your excuse, maybe. Let me tell you to take that gun back to where you got it from, and leave it there. Never you mind how I learned about you. I am keeper on this estate, and I know my duties."

The coolness with which he said this to Harold Sims, in the presence of Billy Lander and Winter, who stood equally as coolly, looking on, completely subdued the self-appointed huntsman. Sims turned and retreated into

126

the forest by the direction from which he had suddenly appeared.

Billy released the Airedale, who also had taken the hint from the wiry older dog. It floundered off after its master, and the party of three resumed the way along the ride, with Rover now in the lead, still somewhat ruffled and indignant.

"That boy took you up sharp, Arthur," said Peter Apps, after they had walked on in silence for some minutes. "Made a fair mark for you, I'd say. What's he got against you?"

Arthur looked shrewdly at the old man and laughed.

"You don't know any more than I do, Peter," he said, as though propounding a double riddle. "Reckon it may be on account of young Tom. They did fall foul at one time, didn't they, Master William?"

"Don't keep mastering me, Arthur," said Billy. "I shall feel you've fallen foul of *me*."

He spoke jokingly, intending not to commit himself one way or the other about Harold Sims.

Nothing more was said on this matter while they came through the woods to the open scrub where the timber had been felled. It was the spot where Arthur and Tom had seen the fallow doe and her fawn. Now the ground between the dry stumps was a carpet of windflowers and primroses and the young tendrils of dog's mercury; a vision of tender colors, with the windflowers hesitating between pink and white as the air moved among their petals. A faint sweetness, hardly a perfume, rose from the carpet.

"That be a pretty sight," said Peter Apps. "I never grow weary of that, year after year. Brings me back a bit, it does, Arthur."

127

He was overheard by Sir George, who with Jeremy Hogg had approached from the road that ran across the top, dividing the open moor from the flower-filled clearing.

"You're the toughest gamekeeper in the country, Apps," cried the Squire, "and here I find you weeping over the windflowers."

"They don't do no harm to my creatures," said Apps, taking the Squire's teasing solemnly. "They don't be our worst enemies."

"Why, what are you getting at?" said Sir George. "Anything amiss?"

Peter Apps became evasive, as is the countryman's habit when asked a direct question. "Well, there's some folk as don't know the rules—new to our ways, like."

"Conundrums, my good man, conundrums!" said Sir George. He turned to his foreman, the carpenter, Jeremy Hogg. "Know anything of this, Jeremy?"

But Jeremy was also a countryman, though in a position of some authority. He, too, covered up, though he had heard the rumor put about by the postman. But the new people at the big house were rich folk and likely to be friendly with the Squire, from whom they had bought the house. He, too, became cautious. Indeed he said nothing, merely shook his head and turned to the business in hand, which was to discuss the ways and means of uprooting the neglected stumps of the oak trees felled ten years ago and of replanting with saplings of a kind yet to be decided.

More than an hour was spent on the clearing, while they paced the ground, argued about the soil, the exposure to the weather, the cost of protection of the young trees against rabbits and other "vermin".

In those days, when the horse was the only power tool in agriculture, the clearing of roots from felled woodland was a slow and laborious job. A gang of men with picks and spades had first to dig around each tree stump, to expose and cut the outlying roots. Then a team of horses had to drag out the root with ropes and chains. After that, the stump and masses of loose roots would be burned on the spot or carted off before the ground could be plowed, and all this was done by horsepower.

These were the jobs first discussed by the Squire and his men, and it was decided that after harvesting was over, in the coming September, work should start on clearing the ground.

"And now I stand for oak," said Arthur Winter. "I reckon you say so, Mr. Hogg?"

Jeremy Hogg, though he agreed about planting oak, did not appreciate being told so by a man of lower rank on the estate. He was silent and bided his time. His frown showed his disapproval of Winter for speaking out of turn. It was the gamekeeper who supported the wood-man.

"Arthur be right, sir," he said to the Squire. "I may be old-fashioned, but I knows the way of my creatures. So long as we have oak woods in our country, we should get good shooting."

And he patted the barrels of his gun affectionately.

"It's a long-term investment, Sir George," said Jeremy Hogg, "but the estate will benefit, and there's no wood grown in this country so good as oak for working with—furniture or building—more general and more lasting than beech." This last remark was added slyly, with a shrewd glance at the Squire, whose preference for beech-wood furniture Hogg had always criticized.

"What do you say, Billy?" asked his father. "Even in your lifetime the investment in oak won't mature. Maybe your grandchildren will benefit."

Billy knew his father and was amused at the solemnity, half-mockery, with which the Squire was debating with the serious-minded countrymen. He knew, too, that there was no real difference of opinion and that his father was merely using the occasion to air the problems and res-ponsibilities of a big landowner.

"I should say, Father"—and he paused in order to impress his listeners—"that a good mixture would be best, and the most suitable will win in the end."

Sir George laughed aloud and turned to Jeremy Hogg.

"There you see, Jeremy! We have a future Prime Minister in the family! And we'll take his advice. Mark my words, and put this on record. In a hundred years from now, your future Squire will be proved right."

"It's a light soil up here on the moor," said Arthur Winter, "but oak will find its own depth, sir. We'd better make it mainly oak, with some ash and beech. I don't go for that spruce, I must say."

"Winter, how d'you think we can pay our way meantime?"

They all knew Sir George was only half serious over this, and nobody answered.

"Well, it shall be so. Billy, it is your plan, your first act in the running of the estate which will one day be your responsibility. There's another thing which makes me follow your choice: a mixed woodland suits my fallow deer, and you all know what that means to me. And this reminds me that I've not yet seen this almost legendary white fawn with which we have been blessed so early in the season."

He turned to Arthur Winter, and added, "I hear young Tom has lost his heart to it, Winter. He's an odd fellow."

"He'll come along all right, sir, if his mother don't coddle him up too much."

With that, the consultation broke up, and Billy went off with his father and Jeremy Hogg to the horse and trap which were waiting up on the road, while Winter and Apps returned to the forest.

"Dang it!" said Peter Apps suddenly. "I was a fool not to let Squire know about that boy walking the woods with his father's gun. Proper danger to the community, he be. But somehow, the words wouldn't come."

"Don't you fret, Peter," said Winter. "Give that young cub a bit of rope, and he'll hang himself in due time."

"Yes, and do a world of damage meanwhile," was the reply.

17 More Provocation

Billy and Tom planned that on the first
Saturday morning of the Easter holidays, a systematic
quartering of the forest should be made, with the purpose
of sighting the doe and her white fawn. They knew that,
for some primitive, instinctive reason, or rather non-
reason, she had not yet rejoined the herd, though the
buck with whom she had mated last autumn had done so.
Somewhere in the forest or up on the moors or along the
open country between the forest and the sea, the doe with
her nursling was roving, cunning to conceal herself and
her infant during this period of self-imposed isolation and
consequent danger. She had broken the laws of the herd
behavior because of the unusual color of her fawn.

"It's always that way," said Billy. "Don't you remember that tiny white squirrel two years ago? It haunted the
lawns at home for a few weeks, and Mother fed it. It had
pink eyes that seemed half-blind. She said it was called an
albino. But it was doomed, first because it was alone and
then for its helplessness. I suppose a fox got it, or a hawk.
Pretty sad, but there it is, you can't go against the
general run of things."

Tom shivered. He found Billy becoming more and
more worldly-wise, and though this impressed him, it also

frightened him, and put up a barrier against the intimacy which had made them like twin brothers, the squire's son and the woodman's son.

"That's not a law of nature," said Tom.

"But it is," said Billy. "That's how things work at school, too. If you're different, you suffer. A good thing for you, Tom, that you don't have to go to boarding school."

"I suppose so," was the moody reply. Tom already had sufficient cause to dislike boarding school, since it had separated him from Billy and was already, after only two terms, subtly changing that Billy. At least, Tom thought so.

This conversation accompanied the first stage of that Saturday morning exploration, which began in the forest. The boys had mapped their course the evening before, sitting at the table in Billy's bedroom up at the Hall, where Tom had been invited to supper by Lady Lander. She treated Tom as one of the family, for his knowledge of wildlife was much to her liking.

The plan was to follow the main rides, which quartered the forest, east and west, north and south, the westerly ride leading to the Hall and the farmland beyond, which joined the open scrub and pasture that reached to the village and turned southeast and east along the sea-shore. The house which Lady Lander called the White Elephant looked over this curve of open country, for it lay south of the Hall, a mile away.

The boys walked through the forest, Tom leading the way, almost unconsciously, up to the spot where he had first seen the white fawn.

"You're very quiet," said Billy, close at his heels. "Nothing wrong, is there?"

"No," said Tom, "nothing wrong. I was thinking."

133

"What about?"

"Oh, I don't know. Can't quite explain it. You being away leaves me alone here."

"Well, it's like old times again now, Tom. Nothing has changed."

"That's not so," said Tom so emphatically that Billy was startled, and instantly decided to say no more about it.

Fortunately, their attention was diverted. They were just emerging from the woods to the clearing, with the moor beyond, when they startled the main herd of deer. The lovely creatures were standing under the trees when the boys disturbed them. Their leader lifted his head and began to trot sedately across the flowered clearing, picking his way without looking down, his head and neck poised as though deliberately, with affection. The herd became conscious of his lead and began to follow, though one or two does hesitated until they had sorted out their fawns, each mother and child then trotting off side by side.

The deer were not greatly disturbed, for Billy had not brought Pembroke, his corgi. He had agreed with Tom that the dog's presence would prevent them from getting near the doe and her fawn, should they sight them. The herd trotted after the leader, rise and fall, rise and fall, picking their way daintily over the windflowers and primroses, leaving no impression of damage to the spring-time carpet. The mild April sunshine heightened the dappling of their coats, giving it a velvet touch.

The contact was so peaceful that one mother and child lingered out of pure curiosity and allowed the boys to approach. Billy hesitated, afraid of scaring them, but he saw Tom move forward, hand outstretched to touch

134

the doe. She allowed this and tossed her head up and down several times, sniffing at Tom's hand. The fawn moved around from her other side, quite fearless, and added a tiny muzzle to that of the mother already exploring the palm of Tom's hand.

Billy watched his friend, awed by the gentleness, the concentration of the motionless figure. It was as though Tom were hypnotized. The group stood thus for several moments, and time ceased. Then, curiosity satisfied, the doe moved off to rejoin the herd, and her fawn leaped around to her other side again, open to fear. Still Tom did not move or drop his hand.

"Wake up, Tom!" said Billy. "They've gone!"

Tom blinked, turned and said sadly, as though whispering to himself, "Yes. They trust me, don't they?"

Billy let that pass.

"No sign of the white one," he said. "They must still be on their own. D'you think the herd has driven them out? I said that was likely to happen."

"Then they might be on the other side of the woods," said Tom. "We *must* find them. You *must* see it, Billy."

"Well, we shall, in due course, if not today," said Billy, rather worried by Tom's intensity. "There's no hurry, is there?"

"I don't know, I don't know," said Tom.

"You're crazy," said Billy, but he spoke good-naturedly as he led the way eastward along the clearing, to find the entrance to a farther ride that would lead them through the eastern reaches of the forest where it ended in open country that ran back from the scrubland along the cliff top.

He studied Tom from time to time, still puzzled by his
136

friend's silence and reserve. "You must have seen a ghost," he said suddenly. "Or what has happened while I've been away?"

Tom stared ahead. "No, it wasn't a ghost. It was real enough!"

"Why," said Billy, now thoroughly bewildered, "you're still thinking of that white fawn. Come along, Tom. It's not so unusual as all that."

"But we must find it." The voice was low, level, determined.

Almost to Billy's relief, they found something else, coming toward them through the woods from the seashore—two figures whom the boys now recognized, Margaret and Harold Sims, with the Airedale on a lead. As they drew near, the Airedale struggled to greet Tom, and Harold jerked him back irritably.

Tom saw Billy flush as Margaret greeted him coolly. She then turned to Tom. "Tell me about it, Tom. We've been looking for it. That's why we've got the dog on the lead. He's still not trained."

"There's nothing wrong with him," said Harold. "I'll prove it. Look, you fellows. Now, boy. Sit! Sit!"

But the released Airedale did not sit. It gamboled around Tom and then lay fawning at his feet, twitching and jerking to attract his attention.

"There, you see!" said Harold. "He's quite obedient."

Before the dog could move, he pounced and put it on the lead again. "We'll join you," he said to Billy. "Which way are you going?"

Tom wanted to cry out to Billy, to prevent him from telling that they were in search of the white fawn. But he kept silent, still with sufficient trust in his friend and foster brother. He was right.

137

"Oh, just stretching our legs," said Billy. "We might as well join forces. Just as well you've got that hound on the lead, with all these young deer about. Old Peter Apps would have a fit if he caught him roaming about in the forest. You remember that encounter the other day!"

"What was that?" asked Tom, neither whose father nor Billy had told of the dog fight in the forest. But Harold Sims was not so reticent. Nor was he even aware of Tom Winter's odd character, which people who knew him tended to protect.

"The gamekeeper's dog attacked him," said Sims. Then he added, "And nearly got itself slaughtered."

He looked at Billy, daring him to question this account. But Billy said nothing. He followed his own principle of "being civil". He was also studying the expression on Margaret's face.

She was the next to speak, and what she said might be interpreted either way. "That's why we've got the fierce brute on the lead."

"I thought it was to keep him from chasing the deer," said Tom.

"You can put it that way, if you like," she said dryly. "It would please the gamekeeper anyway."

"That cantankerous old brute!" said Harold.

"Oh, come!" said Billy mildly. "That's his job, you know. I think he let you off lightly, especially as you had a gun with you."

"Yes, a gun!" said Tom. "I've heard you've been ranging the woods with a gun."

Harold Sims turned on him, as he would not have turned on Billy, the Squire's son. "What of that? I suppose your father told you? I should have thought poachers were more discreet."

"Poacher, did you say poacher?" said Tom, very quietly, as he approached Sims, his fists clenched so tightly that his knuckles shone like ivory.

Margaret stepped between them and took Tom by the arm.

"No," she said. "It's not true, even if it *is* true. Remember what I told you, Tom. It's never worth making trouble with him. I think we'd better go back through the woods, as we intended. I'm sorry, Billy."

Billy flushed again. She seemed always to put a spell on him, reducing him to speechlessness, quite out of character. But he summoned up a few words. "Yes, these two are always at loggerheads. I don't know who is to blame."

"I have my theory," said Margaret. "Come along, Harold. I've got the dog."

Brother and halfsister, with the Airedale between them, walked off, leaving Tom and Billy together, neither able to look at the other. When they were alone, Tom suddenly began to sob, putting his hands to his face.

"Shut up, you fool," said Billy, taking him around the waist. "Can't you see he's as crazy as you are? The pair of you! What d'you expect? Everything to fall into your lap? I tell you, Tom, you may be king of the forest; but you've got to learn to live with the rest of us, and we are not all angels!"

18 Nearer the Vision

It was a fruitless journey, for after the encounter
with Margaret and Harold Sims the boys felt shy of each
other and had little to say during the rest of the morning.
But they continued the search, moving down to the cliffside country and returning that way westward until they
reached the other end of the forest, where they took the
last ride into it, before meeting the road to the village.

They paused at the cross-rides where they had to part,
Billy to return to the Hall and Tom to cut across under
the trees to the ride that led to the back of his house.

"Well, we haven't found it," said Billy.

"No."

"And you've asked for trouble again with that little
hero. I told you before, Tom, that he needs careful
handling."

"That's what his sister said," Tom replied. He was
still upset, angry with himself for having been tricked
into anger, as Sims had intended.

"Oh, well, there are two of us at you," said Billy. "But
when did she tell you that?"

"Oh, when we first met. I forget when it was. Why do
you ask?"

Billy flushed again. "Oh, no reason. But she's been

140

home from school for some days, hasn't she?"

"What of it?" said Tom indifferently.

"You see how she stopped that row," said Billy. "Pretty good stuff there, plenty of nerve."

Tom saw things differently. "Everybody is out to comfort that undersized brute. I wanted to knock his head off for what he said about my father."

"Yes, but you know, Tom, he was in fact right, in a sort of way."

"That's nothing to do with it. He's poking his nose into a world he doesn't understand."

"That's why we've got to teach him."

"Well, it makes me mad."

"So it seems, but you've got a lot to learn, too."

Billy walked away, but he turned, as always, before disappearing round the bend in the ride, put his fingers to his lips and blew a shrill whistle. Tom was reassured, and went home more calmly, though eager as ever to find the white fawn.

After the midday meal Mrs. Winter sent Tom to the village with the basket of clean linen. She laundered every week for the doctor's house, thus adding enough to the housekeeping money to ensure a joint of meat for the Sunday dinner. Tom went alone and reluctantly, for he wanted to continue his search, after the failure that morning. He delivered the clean and collected the dirty linen, then went on to the butcher's shop with the laundry money and bought an aitchbone of beef. The basket hung heavily on the way home, and several times Tom had to set it down and take a few moments' rest, flexing his stiffened arms.

During one of these pauses he heard the sound of hooves. A horse and trap overtook him, coming from the

141

village. Mrs. Sims held the reins, and her son Harold sat beside her. She drove past Tom without any sign of recognizing him. Harold, however, wanted to make sure that his mother should not offer a lift to Tom and his burden. Tom saw him reach behind his mother's back and snatch the whip out of the holder. Raising it above his head, offside of the trap, he gave a smart crack that made the horse shudder nervously and gallop for several paces before relapsing into a trot. Tom heard Mrs. Sims say peevishly, "What *are* you doing, darling? Put the whip back."

Harold obeyed, but not before repeating the performance, though this time the horse was prepared and did not alter its pace. The boy glared over his shoulder to make sure that Tom had taken the hint of derision.

Tom watched the trap disappear before he picked up the basket and trudged on.

By the time he reached home, the afternoon was fad-

ing into evening, the daylight further shortened by heavy clouds which dropped an April shower. Tom was caught in its onset and ran for the last hundred yards along the lane. He had seen the trap standing by the front door of the Sims's house, with a man about to lead the horse away. Tom thought that it must have been left there, in the shafts, for at least a quarter of an hour after Mrs. Sims and Harold alighted. Only the coming of the rain had reminded somebody in the household that the animal needed attention. Tom noticed this and felt it more bitterly than the previous incident of the whip's being flourished almost in his face.

The shower continued, bringing cold air down with the twilight. Tom was tired after the morning's walk followed by the shopping expedition to the village. Even so, he put a sack round his shoulders, and ventured out after tea, if only to try out his boots which had been resoled by Arthur. It was good to feel dry and secure above the thickness of leather. It was not so frequent an experience as to have lost its novelty.

Darkness was not yet complete, and over the open country beyond the lane the shapes of the budding bushes loomed up, shining under the rain. Suddenly the cloud broke in the west, and a haze of delayed light picked out the falling arrows of rain and the wet grasses. Tom leaned over a gate a few yards down from the cottage, and looked along the open sward.

The whole world glittered; the pasture, the bushes, the edge of the forest behind him. He saw the smoke rising from the cottage chimney, ghostly and gray. Gradually the brightness faded, while Tom stood watching. Then, in the distance, from where an arm of the forest jutted out like a windbreak toward the cliff, he saw

143

a movement, a shifting of shadows. It took shape for a moment, then disappeared. But Tom knew what it was. It was the white fawn, touched by the last light as the belated sunset died.

He stood there, clasping the wet top bar of the gate. The rain drummed on the sack around his shoulders, but he did not hear it. He had found what he wanted, though only for a split second. A strange, unaccountable sense of happiness flooded over him, like the warmth from a fire.

"That's her," he said, and it might have been aloud. "Little beauty! That's her."

Without knowing what he was doing, he began to run along the lane, away from home and toward the main road. He must find Billy; he must tell him and bring him out to see the little miracle. He did not notice the darkness but ran on without stumbling, guided and upheld by the fever of excitement. Drunken men are said to be prevented in this way from hurting themselves when they stagger and fall, out of self-control. Some other self takes charge, as it took charge of Tom Winter while he ran through the night and the dwindling rain when the shower gave place to starlight and a bronze eastern glow in the sky behind him, forecast of the rising moon.

At the joining of the roads, by the gateway of the drive into the Sims's house, Tom became breathless. He had lived through a full day; but it was not over yet, and he was not conscious of being tired. Indeed he was elated, triumphant. He did not stop to think that he had been given only a momentary glimpse of the fawn and that it was on the move with its mother and unlikely to be seen again that night. He had only one idea in his mind. Billy must be brought to share this discovery.

As he approached the Hall, his excitement revived and set him running again. He passed the stately front entrance and ran around to the kitchen door in the back courtyard. Pembroke, the corgi, barked and came rushing at the intruder; but he recognized Tom, and the uproar changed from hostility to welcome.

Somebody inside had been warned, however, and the door opened. The cook looked out. "Who's that?" she cried into the night.

"It's me, Tom."

"Why, boy, whatever is the matter?"

"I've seen it! I've seen it! I must tell Billy. Where is he? What's he doing?"

"Come in, Tom. Come in, and calm yourself down, boy. Why, you're all of a sweat. You'll catch your death!"

Tom was at first dazzled by the light on the kitchen table. Then he saw that Billy was kneeling on a chair, at

145

work on a set of model engine parts, which he was filing smooth. There they shone, laid out on spread newspaper under the lamp.

On the other side of the table sat Harold Sims, reading the booklet of instructions for assembling the model.

Both boys stopped their work and looked up in surprise at this mad apparition which had appeared out of the night.

Tom stopped. He had seen Harold beyond the lamp, a figure half in shade. The fever, the wonder, began to ebb away. For a moment Tom could not speak. Then he said haltingly, "I've seen it. Billy."

"Seen what?" said Billy, who was concentrated on the task in hand.

But Tom could not speak out in front of Harold Sims. Misgiving, distrust, made him evasive. "You know," he said. It was an appeal to Billy, coming from the depths of their lives together, the complete understanding.

But now the understanding was blurred; or maybe it was merely that Billy was preoccupied. Tom appealed again.

"Aren't you coming?" He faltered. "If we hurry it will still be there."

"Oh, *that*!" said Billy. "What, tonight? You're crazy, Tom."

He would have said more but thought better of it as he saw across the table, the expression of amused contempt on Harold's face. He temporized, and turned to Tom.

"No! There's no hurry. Stay and give us a hand with this." He indicated with a gesture the metal parts laid out under the lamp.

Tom stared, speechless, and a funny spectacle he made, with his hair lank and the wet sack round his shoulders.

146

Harold Sims began to laugh. It was a cold laughter, like a knife blade flashing in the lamplight.

With a little exclamation, half a groan, half a sob, Tom turned and ran out into the night.

"You said he's crazy," said Harold as the cook shut the door, after peering out at the vanishing figure of Tom Winter. "Why d'you bother with such a fool?"

Billy did not answer. He was annoyed with Tom for creating yet another scene, as always happened when he confronted this newcomer, Harold Sims. And Billy's annoyance conquered his discretion.

"He's no fool," he said. "Tom's like his father, only more so."

"Phew! And what's he on about now?"

Billy hesitated, then gave in. "Oh! It's the white doe," he said. "We couldn't find it when we searched all this morning. But now he says he's seen it. That's why he's in such a state."

Harold had turned his face away from the lamplight, in order to read the small print on the booklet. Billy did not see the sudden gleam of passion in the boy's eyes or the movement of the tongue over the lips, as though about to taste a dainty dish.

19 *A Friend in Need*

Tom Winter did not run home. He was defeated, and even his physical strength collapsed. He felt sick in his stomach. Billy had failed him. Of that he was certain.

Slowly, dragging one foot after the other, he walked through the darkness along the road from the Hall. He was not even able to think. A sense of betrayal covered him, deeper than the darkness of the night; much deeper, for the world around him was now touched by slanting moonlight, and the sky was alive with stars. He did not hear the drip of the recent rain as its crystals dropped from the twigs and buds above his head. He was both blind and deaf within his cloud of misery.

He reached the lane turning off past the gates of the Sims's house, hateful to him now. The moon faced him, well up over the open country and the sea. A long run of quicksilver over the water glittered, heavy and sullen as the unrest in his mind. Loneliness, friendlessness— that was the signature of the night.

"Tom," he heard, without hearing. He was trudging on, but again his name greeted him. He looked up, dully, slowly, and saw Margaret Sims standing by the gate.

"I had to come out," she said. "After the rain I had to come out and smell things. Oh, isn't it heaven!"

Then she saw that something was wrong. She leaned forward, peering anxiously at him. "What is it, Tom? What's the matter?"

Tom did not answer. He began to move on, but Margaret darted forward, and the mackintosh flung loosely around her shoulders fell to the ground. Her dress shone white in the moonlight. She touched him, and he tried to shake her hand off his arm.

"Tell me, what has happened?"

Tom put his arm across his face, struggling with himself.

"Nothing! Nothing!" he said, his voice shaken with anger and broken pride.

"You've come from the Hall! You've seen Harold," said Margaret, almost whispering. "Tell me, Tom, I know! I understand! But you must—"

"There's nothing to tell," he said, removing his arm from his face. "I went up to fetch Billy, to bring him to see the white fawn. It's down at the other end of the woods. I saw it just now. Just now—no, long ago, at sunset. I can't tell. I can't think."

"I'll come with you," said Margaret. "I'll fetch my coat. Look, I've dropped it. One moment, Tom. I'll come with you."

He stared at her. "You can't," he said. "You'll get into trouble."

"Nonsense!" she cried bitterly. "Nobody cares what I do."

She took her place beside him, and they walked on, both silent, Margaret waiting for him to speak, Tom unable to, unwilling to, because this girl was Harold Sims's sister, and he could not trust her. At that moment he trusted nothing. The moon and stars were treacheous.

But Margaret was patient. She had learned the hard way, to wait and to watch.

They reached the gate over which Tom had leaned and where he had known the vision which he had been seeking for weeks. Instinctively Tom stopped there.

"It was here," he said, breaking the long silence.

"I think I know," she whispered. "I think so. You've seen it again?"

"Yes," he said, but the tone of his voice implied that it meant nothing now. It had been spoiled.

"You ought to go in for your supper," said Margaret. "You're all shaking, Tom. You've done enough for one day. Besides, if we go on, we are not likely to see it again. It will have gone."

They stood at the gate, however, peering along the moon path over the open country and the sea. But all was motionless, except for the heavy flecks of quicksilver in the water. There was no other sign of life. Even the dripping of raindrops from the trees had ceased.

"It will come back again," said Margaret.

Tom shook his head.

"You haven't told me what happened, Tom."

"There's nothing to tell," he said, still irritable and desperate. "Your brother was there with Billy. I couldn't speak in front of him. But Billy knew what I meant." He paused, struggling with himself, then said hoarsely, "He wasn't interested. He wasn't!"

"Oh, you're so stupid, Tom! But don't I know? I've had to learn. I live with them, Harold and his mother. It's no use expecting anything. Why should you worry? If it's Billy, then you are wrong. He's not unfair. It's the other way. He tries to be too fair. And he's so interested in *things*. Was he working on his new craze, the railway engine? I've heard all about that. You've known him all your life and should understand his ways—how he concentrates on one thing, then another. I've seen that already. And he loves to talk, which is more than you do, Tom Winter!"

She put her arm around his shoulders and gave him a shaking. "It's time you went home," she said. "And I'll come with you, to make sure."

They could smell the woodsmoke from the cottage chimney before they turned the bend in the lane that would reveal the building. They heard the trundle of a barrow and saw Tom's father come round from the

151

woodstack with a load of small logs to the front door, which gave straight into the living room.

"Ah! there you are, Tom," he cried; then, seeing the companion, "Why, miss, you out as well? That's not so seemly, I'd say."

"I've just come to see Tom home from our front gate."

"Well, get you in and have a bite with us. 'Tis just mealtime." Then he added with a chuckle, "And legitimate fare!"

"No, Mr. Winter, thank you," said Margaret. "They'll expect me at home. I only came out to smell the springtime, and Tom was passing. So I kept him company. And he's got good news, haven't you, Tom?"

She said this deliberately and with emphasis, daring Tom to indulge in his misery and sense of defeat.

"Why, what's that?" asked Arthur, indulgent toward the young people.

"I saw it," said Tom. He spoke with reluctance, as though he did not believe his own words. Then, with more vigor and a return of confidence, "Yes, Dad. The little fawn. It was right up at the end of the trees, where the pasture turns inland. But daylight was failing."

"Well, I'll be blessed," said Arthur. "So we've traced it at last. You'd better let young William know. He'll want to see it, and so will the Squire."

There was a long silence. Then Tom stooped and began to gather an armful of the tiny logs.

"Good night, Mr. Winter. Good night, Tom," said Margaret. She hesitated for a moment, then decided to say no more. Hitching her coat up over her shoulders, she walked off up the lane, as bold as a soldier.

Arthur looked at the diminishing figure. "That be a good lass," he said. "Ah, a pity, a pity."

But he did not explain what he meant.

20 Morning Service

Sunday was a day of torture for Tom Winter. He wanted to shut himself away from everybody, but he had to go with his parents to church, and he knew whom he would see there.

Surely enough, there sat Sir George and Lady Lander, and Billy on the other side of his mother. Their pew was large, with tall sides that made it like a cabin, opposite the pulpit and at right angles to the pews in the nave and aisles. This gave the occupants a clear view of the congregation in the nave and the south aisle. Billy's face was bright, a replica of his father's. Both were serene, benevolent, at peace with the world.

The Winter family sat in the third pew in the south aisle, near the pulpit and, as the village church was small, Tom and Billy were only a few yards apart, almost facing each other. Tom hung his head, trying not to catch a glance from Billy's eye. But his anger, nursed overnight and multiplied into all manner of grievances, forced him to look furtively across the church. Billy, in spite of his air of easy indifference, was sharp enough to intercept that sullen scowl from his friend. He gave a slow-motion wink, a wink on tiptoe, suitable to the place and occasion.

This made Tom more disturbed than ever. It implied

that Billy was not even aware of the wound he had
inflicted last night. It, therefore, put Tom in the wrong,
as taking offense without cause. The expression on Tom's
face was such that his mother nudged him to remind him
where he was. Tom's face flushed with the effort to
control his feelings. He turned at a slight angle, as far as
he dared, toward the stained-glass window at the farther
end of the pew. He was thus staring at one of the several
monuments to vanished Landers. This one showed a
knight and his wife kneeling in prayer, face to face, with
four boys behind the father and three girls behind the
mother, all wearing seventeenth-century clothes, with
stiff ruffs round their necks. They, too, were serene, like
their last descendant, Billy Lander, whose present calm-
ness now infuriated poor Tom. Fear was the wind that
fanned those grievances into flame. He had known this

155

was coming, from the moment he first heard that Billy was going away to boarding school. Tom stood half-turned toward the wall, one leg twitching nervously. He felt another prod from his mother. She leaned over and whispered, like a ventriloquist, from closed lips, "Behave yourself!" Even his father looked down, inquiringly, fumbling with a prayer book.

Tom concealed himself behind *Hymns Ancient and Modern*, and from this cover took another glance across the nave. There, in the second row, he saw the Sims family, or rather Mrs. Sims, very fashionable, with Margaret on one side of her and Harold on the other. Both were stiff in their Sunday clothes. Margaret's chin was indented by the elastic from her hat. Harold's posterior was conspicuous below an Eton jacket. But that schoolboy garment did not prevent him from looking grown-up. Those quick eyes missed nothing and approved of nothing. They had seen Tom Winter, and in the dim sacred light they glittered but gave no sign of recognition.

Tom's self-torture was thereby doubled. He was confronted with two kinds of indifference: Billy's oblivious, Harold's intentional.

The service proceeded—the psalms, the sermon, the hymns. All passed over Tom's head. He was nailed down in his own misery, a load which had increased overnight.

Then came the organ solo and the agony of walking out, with the likelihood, indeed, the certainty, of being greeted outside by the Squire, who made a regular practice of having a word with such of his estate workers who came to church. No doubt the Simses, those newcomers, would walk away without addressing themselves to anybody other than the Squire and the vicar who stood in the porch.

But Tom was not to escape so easily. Followed by the last strains of the organ, the Winters stepped out into the bright sunshine. Tom blinked, and there before him stood Margaret Sims. She had left her mother talking with Lady Lander. Harold waited alone, bored by all this social affability. But as soon as Margaret left him, he joined Billy, thus preventing him from approaching Tom.

"Are you better this morning, Tom?" said Margaret. "You *were* in a state last night."

"I don't know what you mean," he said, turning to read a tombstone.

"Oh, yes, you do. But please don't include me in it."

"In what?"

"Your private war. Or if you do, count me in with you."

Tom looked at her and realized that she was the first person whom he had openly looked at and recognized since that humiliating moment yesterday evening in the kitchen up at the Hall.

"Thank you," he said, then stood silent and uncomfortable.

"You need not thank me. I've done nothing. But I know what you feel. I live with it!"

"Oh, him!" said Tom. He could not say anything about Billy.

The person referred to now approached, followed by Billy, who may have suggested a word with Tom and Margaret.

Tom looked round for his parents. He wanted to escape, but they were talking to the vicar still, along with Peter Apps and his wife, a little cluster of old-fashioned humanity around the church door.

Margaret stood beside Tom as Harold joined them, or rather it was Billy who joined them, for Harold stood sideways, prepared to pass on.

"Hello you," said Billy. "Hello Margaret. Another service over. What's to do this afternoon? Too good to waste, a day like this."

He was easy still, but not quite at his best. Something about Margaret seemed always to disturb him. She looked at him severely and said, "Don't say it!"

He was shocked by her coldness. He knew at once what she meant. But her plea was too late. He recalled what he had told Harold last night. "Look here—" he wanted to explain; but Harold broke in. He, too, knew what Margaret meant. Opposition always woke his cold temper. He spoke now while looking at Tom. His voice was clear and deliberate.

"Good hunting! Is that what you suggest, Billy? I'm ready for that!"

Margaret stood between him and Tom. She took a step nearer to her brother, to cover him. "You're thinking of rabbits," she said.

"No, I'm not."

"Then you'd better tell Sir George what you have in mind."

He stood glaring at Margaret for a moment. Then, with an exclamation of disgust, he walked away to join his mother, who was moving off with Sir George and Lady Lander toward the carriage waiting beyond the lych-gate. Before he was out of earshot, however, he turned and cried to Billy, his voice loaded with venom, "You need not bring your beater this afternoon."

The three young people stood in amazement, watching him disappear through the lych-gate, to join his mother and Sir George and Lady Lander. They heard the carriage drive off, the horse's hooves clip-clopping along the road, under the churchyard wall.

"Did you hear what he said?" Billy spoke incredulously. "What's got into him, Margaret? He must be crazy, too."

"He is well informed." she said. "He knows about the white fawn and has got the idea into his head that Sir George will want to get rid of it."

"That was my doing," said Billy. "I told him last night, after Tom looked in. He really cornered me, you know. I lost my nerve, Tom, when you turned and ran. Whatever made you behave like that?"

"You weren't interested. That's why."

Tom was still hurt, and he showed it.

"That's not true," said Billy quietly. For the first time, he realized what had upset his friend. "You ought to know me better than that. I was dealing with something

else. I can only do one thing at a time, Tom. I'm sorry. That's all I can say."

He spoke as if bewildered by the whole business—Tom's anger, Margaret's indignation, Harold's cold violence. He looked sadly at the boy and the girl, so clearly united against him.

"There's such a thing as being too easygoing," said Margaret. "Especially when you're dealing with my brother. He needs to be held at arm's length!"

"Oh, I say, that's a bit much, Margaret. I get on all right with him."

"Yes, you'd get on all right with a man-eating tiger."

This reduced Billy to even deeper bewilderment. Tom followed up Margaret's shrewd remark. "If he is going out this afternoon, we ought to be around. He's not to be trusted."

"I think that would be wise," said Margaret. "Once he gets one of these vindictive moods, he's dangerous."

"You certainly have riled him from the day you first met him," said Billy to Tom. "It's cat and dog."

"That's not fair to cat or dog," said Margaret. "They both have natural instincts."

"That's how you feel, is it?" said Billy. "Well, there must be something in it. I suppose we'd better be on the lookout if he's got some mad notion in his head. That was a nasty remark about the beater."

It seemed that Billy had only just realized the evil in that remark, or permitted himself to, for in the first place it was he who had warned Tom that Harold Sims had a long memory.

"Look, Margaret," said Billy, "Harold seems to expect me to go with him this afternoon. I don't want to. The best thing is for me not to be at home. I'll go back with

160

Tom and have dinner there, eh, Tom? Your mother will put up with me for once. Then he and I will prowl about during the afternoon on the watch for trouble. You can let him know that I've done this. It may put him off altogether, and I hope it will. He's not likely to come rout me out from Tom's home."

This practical suggestion restored Tom's confidence in his friend. The cloud partially lifted from his mind—only partially, because Harold Sims had brought the knowledge of evil into his life, something which he had not found in nature, although it was said "to be red in tooth claw."

"But what about your Sunday suit?" asked Margaret. She, too, had forgiven him.

"Oh, I forgot that! Well, I'll cut along home, change my clothes, and come down to the cottage immediately after dinner, before Harold has time to seek me out."

"And I shall come, too," said Margaret. "I'll wait to see if he goes off by himself, and then I'll join you. The trouble is, if he's determined to find the doe and the fawn, sure enough he'll be lucky, though Tom has been looking for weeks without success. That's the way Harold's made. The Devil looks after his own."

Tom remembered how she had tried to plead with him for her brother, and he reminded her of it.

"Yes, but I know him well enough, and the signs of danger. He then needs protection from himself, and there's nobody to do it. Father is always at a board meeting." She did not even mention the boy's mother.

21 Reconnaissance

Sunday dinner was late, because Mrs. Winter had been to church and the potatoes had to be boiled when she got home. The joint of beef, cooked overnight, was to be eaten cold. That made it "go further", as Mrs. Winter maintained. She thus had it both ways, economically and religiously. But her husband raised no objection to this weekend habit. He respected his wife's devotion to the church and took her frequent criticisms of his easy ways and of what she called Tom's "wildness" with good-natured tolerance.

The woodman, wife and son sat at the table in the living room, and Arthur began to carve.

"You know, Mother," he said, while handling the knife with masterly skill, "I've still got no strength back in this arm. How long is it going to be afore I'm a good man-about again? Jerks me up, it does, just carving a joint of meat."

"Go on with you, Arthur Winter," she said, with her back turned to her man. She was about to serve the vegetables from the saucepans, which stood on the stove after the water had been poured off. The oven door was half open to prevent the Yorkshire pudding from burning. Plenty of extras made the meat "go even further."

"You're as good as the next of them, but you lack patience."

She came to the table, saucepan in one hand and serving spoon in the other. She looked at Tom critically, as though about to accuse him of lacking patience also. But what she saw made her say, "Why! Whatever! You been and changed your Sunday suit! What's that mean, young man, on a day of rest?"

Tom glanced at his father for help, but Arthur was too wily. He bent with redoubled attention over the joint of beef.

"I'm taking care of it, Mother," said Tom most solemnly.

Arthur coughed, to smother laughter. "Dang that," he said. "I made a job of it, but it pays that arm of mine, I tell you."

Mrs. Winter was not to be sidetracked.

"That's not like you, Tom Winter," she said. "I've not known you so careful, ever in your young life. Now tell me what's brewing!"

"Oh, well," said Tom, "it's like this. Since Dad and I saw that doe with her white fawn, I've wanted to show it to Billy; only they've kept out of sight. But I spotted them yesterday, right over the farther side of the woods, for a flash, just before dark. Billy and I arranged after church this morning to take a quiet walk along the cliffs. They're in that part, and we may get a glimpse of them again. He's not seen them yet."

Mrs. Winter listened, gravely suspicious, while she piled the potatoes and cabbage on the plates of roast beef, then drew the pan of Yorkshire pudding out of the oven and returned with it to the table.

"Just a walk then, is it? None of that wild traipsing

163

about in the woods? That's no occupation for a Sunday."

"Oh, no, Mother," said Tom religiously.

He was lighthearted again, surer of himself after learning to understand Billy more calmly and trustfully. He looked across the table at his father and saw a pair of innocent blue eyes that shared the conspiracy. Behind Arthur's slow woodman's ways, there lurked a quick wit. Tom knew at once what the scrutiny meant. It as good as said, "Tell me later."

"Well, I don't know," said Mrs. Winter. "But we'll say grace."

She looked to the head of the house, and he demurely

obeyed. Then they set to on the good English fare, the great feast of the week.

That course was followed by a baked rice pudding and homemade plum jam.

"Phew!" said Arthur at the end of the meal. "I be properly filled up. I reckon on a nap or maybe a short walk to shake it down like!"

"You men!" cried Mrs. Winter. "Who's to help me with the washing up? Not a soul, I suppose!"

"No, Mother. That's wrong! Tom and I will wipe and put away, then you can go upstairs and get your legs off the ground. A quiet nap will do you good."

Whether or not Mrs. Winter suspected that something was afoot, she agreed to Arthur's wheedling suggestion. After all, it was the usual Sunday practice to give her a hand. Arthur wiped, and Tom put the plates, knives, forks and spoons away. He could have done it blindfolded. He knew every inch of the cottage, just as he knew the rides of the forest behind it and the long stretch of open country above the cliffs in front of it. We all cover our own territory with the microscope of habit, a strange, but unerring faculty.

Both father and son were conspirators. Arthur suspected that Tom and Billy had some project in mind, and being young in heart, he wanted to share the adventure. The object in helping Mrs. Winter clear up after Sunday dinner was more complicated than usual, so that Mrs. Winter should go for what she called "a lie-down" on Sunday afternoon, the only time in the week when she permitted herself this indulgence. Today, father and son, unconfessed to each other, had another reason for wanting her out of the way.

When they were alone in the kitchen, Arthur subdued

165

his hearty voice to a whisper. "What d'you be up to, you young rascals? Proper couple of poachers, you do seem."

Tom was perplexed, but after some quick thinking, he said, "We don't trust Harold Sims. He's up to some game with that gun and dog. There's wrong in him, Dad. He took against us from the start, you and me. But I reckon he's against everybody, everything. His sister has warned us, too."

"Yes, but what's worrying you, boy? That young ignoramus can't touch us. He's but a town lad and knows nothing of our ways."

"Ask Billy about that, Dad. He says Sims is a quick learner and cunning with it."

"Is that so?" said Arthur. "Maybe I'd better be around, too, if he be up to his tricks. Pity Squire ever let that place go to these strangers. Old Peter Apps said so at the beginning. He don't like his preserves spied on and trampled over. But what do you reckon this boy be up to?"

Tom hesitated. He was shy of talking about the white fawn.

"Oh," he said vaguely, "we just have the feeling that he may be out on his own. He said something to Billy about 'good hunting', and that put us on the alert."

"That's a matter for Peter Apps, Tom. I think I'll tell him of this. You and William, likely, would do better on your own. Peter and I might well be out unbeknown like, to join you if need be."

Tom agreed, though he was not sure that he and Billy welcomed interference from grown-ups. They were liable to take charge when things became really interesting.

"You'll leave us to it, Dad?" he said.

Arthur nodded. It was a trustworthy nod. "You better get along then, Tom. Mind you, 'tis the woods as come

166

first. The livestock must be protected. Up to that point, we won't bother you."

Tom looked at the American wall clock in its maple-wood case. At that moment it gave three throaty strokes, like cheers. The afternoon was passing, but all was fair out-of-doors. The sun shone, billowing isolated clouds floated, dropping their silver shadows on the sea and patches of dullness over the young green of the forest. Light was deceptive, capricious.

Tom went out by the garden gate, knowing that Billy would come through the woods directly from the Hall. He waited for a few minutes at the junction of the rides, too impatient to pay more than passing attention to the shouting of thrushes and fluting of blackbirds, music that at another time would have stirred his blood and made him want to join in the chorus.

He did, however, notice the distant call of the cuckoo, the first of that season. It was elusive, vanishing, very lonely. He listened for it again, and it was repeated, but farther off, colder, with a touch of mockery.

Billy appeared around the bend of the ride, and seeing Tom, he put his cupped hands to his mouth and blew through his joined thumbs, a perfect imitation of the cuckoo.

"Hear that?" he cried. "I'll bring it again." He repeated his performance as he joined Tom, and sure enough, the reply came through the woods, but from still another direction.

"Is it the same one, Tom?" he cried, all his attention given to this petty incident.

"We'd better move on," said Tom, his impatience aggravated by Billy's lack of purpose.

"Don't fuss," said that worthy. "You'll die young,

167

so solemn and worried. You take that fellow too seriously. We'll find him, if he's out. He can't escape us. He's as clumsy as a sheep."

They had planned to lurk in the forest, thinking that Sims would want to keep undercover if he were out with a gun. They followed this plan, and for nearly an hour they quartered the rides, watching the change of light as the sun moved round, lower toward the west. Cloud shadows still chased each other, penetrating the greenery above and veiling the patches of bluebell and primrose as they passed overhead. Trees appeared and disappeared; everything seemed to be on the move.

"Visibility a bit shaky," said Billy. "He ought to be on top of us before we spot him."

"That works both ways, and in our favor, for we know the country sounds. This breeze will prevent him from hearing us. He's not learned the language of the trees, the bushes and the grass."

"My word, Tom, that sounds pretty fanciful. What an odd fish you are! I'll never know you properly. You come out with these sayings like somebody from the Old Testament."

Tom looked solemn as Billy teased him. They walked on to the top of the woods and rested there awhile. The sun was getting low, and its rays flooded across the moor, making it appear artificial, like a theater set, everything sharply defined.

"No sign of him," said Billy. "We'd better get through to the seashore. If you saw the doe there yesterday at this time, she may have led her fawn there again today. They get into habits."

Tom agreed, and they followed through a farther ride to the eastern end of the forest. The sense of the afternoon's waning made them hurry, and they were breathless when they came to the open country. Here, too, the light was dazzling. The sun was likely to go down in blinding light, a windy setting, with the clouds scattering above the sea and pocking it with silver reflections.

"Impossible to see a thing in the dazzle," said Billy.

"Yes. It looks as though we shall have no luck. Sims may have been boasting with no intention of coming. Or his people may have stopped him. What's his father like?"

"Oh, he's tough, I should say. But he's seldom there— one of those people who are always sitting on committees, or attending board meetings."

"I can't see why they want to take a house in the country," said Tom. He was about to enlarge on this point, when he stopped suddenly, held up his hand to silence Billy, and peered ahead.

"Look!"

22 Into Battle

Tom's voice was hushed. Billy turned to him and saw his face, pale and intense, but lit by the western sunlight, his cheekbones shining where the skin was drawn tight. His eyes were bright, too, wide open and staring.

"Oh, no! Yes, it is!" said Billy, following Tom's pointing hand.

There, in the distance, was the doe. She was quietly grazing, some quarter of a mile away, just out of the cover of the woods, but in sunlight. She was silhouetted

170

against it, though her dappled gray coat was plainly distinguishable.

"She can't be alone," whispered Billy.

The doe moved slowly as she grazed farther out into the open, toward the cliff.

"She hasn't lost it, has she, Tom?"

Tom did not answer. He shaded his eyes, studying the distant creature, desperately afraid, because he knew the dangers besetting the white fawn, especially, as was probable, its defective eyesight.

"No sign?" Billy was the only one able to speak. He, too, was searching, hands shading eyes.

"It's there!" said Tom at last. "See? It's come across from the trees. It's joined her now. It's sucking. Look, Billy!"

It was a peaceful scene.

"What shall we do?" said Billy.

The answer was provided for them. Out of the trees, obviously following from where the mother and fawn had come through the forest, a human figure crept. He was almost invisible, and he picked his way with some skill, skulking along in the lengthening shadow of the trees, outposts of the forest.

"Who is it, Tom?"

"Who *can* it be? Sims!"

"What's he going to do? Look! He's got that dog on a leash!"

"And he's trying to shoot at the same time! Billy, quick, we must run!"

But the doe was quicker. She looked up, suspicious, tossed her head, and began to run toward the west. The fawn, surprised at its meal, stood splay-legged for a moment, then bounded after its mother.

171

At that, Harold Sims, clumsily handicapped by holding his dog on the lead, raised the gun and fired.

The sound broke the peace of the countryside. It echoed back from the forest, and the reverberations died away along the open country.

The doe and fawn were startled into swiftness. The boys saw them coursing through the scrubland, and they, too, began to run. But Harold Sims appeared to be intoxicated by the excitement of the chase and enraged by the failure of his shot. He unleashed the dog, which bounded forward, howling. The doe and fawn disappeared, still running westward in the direction of the little gully where the small side stream came out to the sea after leaving its parent farther up the estuary, where the village and fishing jetty stood.

Sims was too far away to hear, but Tom shouted, wasting breath as he ran. He was possessed, too, but in a different way. Billy followed, then caught up with him.

"The fool," he said. "We'll make him pay for this. He must be mad!"

Tom wasted no more breath. He rushed on, Billy beside him. They saw Sims waving the gun above his head and cutting across the open toward the cliffside. He appeared to be unaware of the approaching figures.

The voice of the Airedale in full cry could be heard, dwindling westward. It almost vanished as the dog followed the scent down into the gully, and turned seaward. No sign of the deer.

The light, as the sun lowered, became more dazzling, but the boys could see Sims, a dark blotch against the blaze, and they made toward it.

"What's he up to?" gasped Billy. "He's making for the edge!"

He was indeed at the cliff edge when he was forced to stop and, turning, saw Tom and Billy. They drew nearer and saw his face. It was contorted with excitement, the mouth drawn, the eyes blazing: an evil sight.

"Go back! Go back!" he shouted. "You'll spoil my hunt!"

"Put that gun down!" cried Billy. "D'you hear me, Sims? Put that gun down!"

But Sims held it to the ready, dangerously pointing at the boys. Whether or not he intended to fire will never be known, for in turning, he hovered, back to the cliff edge, and stamped with rage. The turf beneath his feet gave way, and a long lozenge of soil began to slip. Sims staggered, floundered, tossed his arms above his head in the effort to keep his balance. He must have had his finger on the trigger, for there was another explosion, whose echo from the woods was lost in a longer, heavier sound, as Harold Sims disappeared over the edge. The gun fell clear and remained in sight, the barrels just over the broken soil.

"Take care, Tom; more of it may go. Lie down and look over."

Tom, suddenly calm, stretched himself out a few feet away, where the edge was still unbroken.

"What's happened?" said Billy, picking up the gun.

"It's getting dark down there," said Tom. "Yes, there he is. He's got caught on a ledge, about halfway down. His coat's over his head, and there's a hawthorn. It's holding him, Billy. It's pierced his shirt, and it's holding him."

"Is he moving?"

"No. He's not moving."

"What do we do?"

"Father and Mr. Apps are out. Dad said they'd be around. We must get them."

As he spoke, a new arrival appeared. Margaret Sims came running along the path that skirted the west end of the forest to join that which led down the gully to the sea and inland up to the lane by her home.

"I know! I know!" she said. "I've tried to follow him. It's Father's gun, but nobody said Harold must not have it. I heard him fire it, and came to—" Then she saw the broken edge of the cliff and Tom lying full length, peering down. She put her hands to her face and shuddered.

Then she quickly recovered and approached Tom, ignoring Billy, who stared at her in dismay.

"Tell me, Tom. May I look? Yes, he's there. I'll go down to him."

"No, you won't," said Tom roughly. "I'm having a look at the cliff. It's not very safe, but I see my way."

Billy had been examining the gun. "He must have reloaded after releasing the dog. There's one cartridge left. I'll fire it, and that may bring Apps and your father, Tom."

"But what can I do?" cried Margaret. "I must help."

"Hadn't you better go home and tell your people?" said Billy, raising the gun and firing it into the air toward the woods.

"No, I'm staying," said Margaret.

"But we must have some rope," said Tom. "You'd better go, Billy. Our shed is the nearest, and you may meet the others on the way. You'll have to hurry, for the light is going. Bring a lantern, too, in case."

"Oh, Tom, what are you doing?" said Margaret.

"He doesn't look very secure there," said Tom. "But the ledge widens beside that bush. If I can get down to that, I can draw him farther onto it. You see he's held only by that branch through his clothes."

Billy left the gun on the grass and set off at a run into the woods, for he knew the path that cut through the edge of them out to the end of the cul-de-sac of the lane where the woodman's cottage stood.

"Now you take my place here, Margaret, and watch as I go down. Keep a lookout for loose bits. Don't stand up, whatever you do. More of that stuff may come away. That's it. Can you see down?"

Margaret obeyed instructions. "Yes, I can see him, Tom. He's not moving."

"We don't want him to move. His life depends on that."

"He's . . . he's still alive then?"

Tom didn't answer. A sudden spasm of hatred flashed through his mind. Then he was calm. Everything became impersonal. He had no feelings, only a sense of something practical to be done.

"I'm going down now," he said. He took a few paces, stamping along the edge, trying its firmness. Some twenty feet along, westward, he stopped. There was a break in the edge, around a cleft that dropped diagonally toward the ledge where the hawthorn was firmly rooted. The cleft was lipped with exposed rock, outcrops from the subsoil, and the main limestone formation.

"This is it," he said, half to himself and half to reassure Margaret. She needed no such encouragement, however. She, too, had grown calm. Tom took a last look at her, the long legs stretched out, the face overhanging the cliff. The sunlight was cooling now, to a rosy tint that softened the girl's figure. Down below, shadows deepened. Tom would have to feel his way.

"I hope they bring lanterns," he said as he groped for his first footing over the cliffside.

"Is it all right, Tom?"

He grunted. "Yes. I'm going down."

Step by step, grasping every available object with his hands, he began to descend along the fissure in the cliff. Every few steps were marked by Margaret's inquiry, but her voice was so calm that it gave him assurance.

"That's right," he said once, when he was about half-way toward his object. But he spoke too soon. He put one foot on a bit of rock that came away. It went rattling down the fissure, bounding from side to side, struck the ledge and bounced up, almost hitting the shapeless figure impaled on the hawthorn bush.

"Oh, no!" cried Margaret, as Tom slipped. But he

recovered, and she was angry with herself for showing alarm. "Sorry, Tom," she said. "Are you all right? I didn't mean that."

But Tom was concentrating. He had the sensation of shrinking his body a little, hardening it by his willpower into a more subtle instrument. He went gingerly now, trusting not a single foothold until he had kicked it before putting his weight on it.

"Has he moved?" he called up.

"What did you say?" Her voice sounded far off, and Tom peered up, to see that by some miracle he had climbed inward and was overhung by the cliff above him. He was frightened by his achievement and rested for a few moments to regain confidence. Looking down, he saw that he would now have the slope in his favor. But that recess above meant that Sims had fallen for several yards in mid air, before landing on the ledge.

The realization flashed across Tom's mind as he prepared to go down. It was not likely that Sims had moved, and Tom did not repeat his question.

23 *Victory*

Though the slope was now in his favor, Tom was still on hazardous ground. The surface was covered with loose shale, and he had to cling to the rock face, every possible knobbly excrescence, while testing with his feet every inch of the descent. A constant flow of shale accompanied him, piling up on the ledge below and bounding over it to plunge into the sea, still farther down, sickeningly far down.

"Tom! Tom!" It was Margaret, losing her nerve and imploring him. But the knowledge that she was there helped him. It made him careful, deliberate.

"It's getting dark down here," he called up, pausing again after another slip owing to the treacherous footing. "Can you see us both, Margaret?"

"Yes, but the light's going. What shall I do, Tom?"

"Stay where you are. That helps."

He started down again, inch by inch, past tufts of samphire and sea lavender. He found that if he trod on or near these shrubs, the footing was more stable.

"Can't see much now," he called. "Any sign of the others?"

"No, not yet. I'm waving my handkerchief. They may not see me lying down."

178

"Wish they'd come. This is pretty heavy going, without a rope."

"They must be here soon, Tom. They can't be far away. Are you sure of your footing?"

"It's rather shaky, but I'm taking care."

The conversation gave him courage. It was thinking aloud and gave the operation an everyday quality, just something to be done without any overexcitement. But he knew the danger. He could feel the threat coming up through his boots, the unsteadiness in his legs.

"Am I really near, Margaret?"

Her voice was still more remote. "Yes. He's down to your right. It looks from here to be only a few yards."

Her voice was drowned by a sudden avalanche of shale that began to carry Tom with it. He threw up his arms to a rift in the rock and steadied himself by gripping there, while the scree flowed for several moments under him.

"I'm all right," he cried. "I see my way now. Don't worry."

He was right. The disturbance subsided, and Tom let himself go slowly, easing out from the handgrip on the rift and finding another lower down. A firmer footing followed, and it lasted for the rest of the drop down to the ledge.

"I've made it," he shouted.

"Oh, Tom."

"Yes, safe enough now. Room to turn around."

"Can you do anything."

"Not sure yet. I'm afraid of the tree breaking away, but it seems firmly rooted. The branch is right up through his shirt. I'm going to try to get an arm around his body and pull him in. He's hanging over the edge now. That branch has saved him."

"But will it hold?"

That was the doubt. It made Tom hesitate. He looked down at the sea, which played over the rocks some hundred feet below. The music of it was in his ears, insistent, a rhythm of warning or evil invitation. He could interpret it either way, as he examined the position of the figure lying half over the ledge. For the first time since he began to climb down the cliff, Tom recalled that this was Harold Sims, the hostile stranger, who had come into his life by some unlucky chance.

It was a dreadful debate, though it lasted for only a few seconds, during the uncertainty about the next step. He dared not look at the boy. His gaze went farther, out to sea.

Something was happening there. From westward, where the gulf spread out to the open over a stretch of sand, there came the sound of a dog barking. A moment later, Tom saw the doe, with the fawn behind her, leaping across the sand. She took to the water and then waited there, paddling, while the white fawn halted, frightened of the strange element. But the barking persisted, and the Airedale could now be seen, still on the scent and approaching the fawn.

The little creature took the plunge, and Tom saw the pair swimming out to sea.

"The dog!" he cried. "The dog! It's chased them into the sea. They'll drown, Margaret. They'll drown!"

"No, Tom, they'll turn back. Don't look! They'll turn back!"

Tom saw the tiny objects in the sea and the dog running up and down along the sands. But he saw no hope of their being saved. He turned to the inert shape of the

boy who had been the cause of all this. Instantly, he knew
what to do.

He now lay down on the ledge and inched his body
forward, until he could grasp the gnarled trunk of the
hawthorn bush with his right arm. The wood was firm
enough, though only a few inches thick.

"Now!" he said, not knowing that he was talking
aloud or that he was acting above himself, under some
outside guidance, as all living creatures do in moments
of crisis.

Peering through the twigs of the bush, he saw the
swimmers veering westward, along the coast and not
straight out to sea. He had the illusion that they were
waiting for him.

He reached forward, still grasping the hawthorn, and
put out his left arm to take Harold Sims around the waist.
The figure was foreshortened, away from him. He had to
strain, leaning farther out, almost over the rim of the
ledge. He felt the bush quiver. But another effort was

needed. He dare not drag the boy in by the legs. The whole setup might collapse.

At last he succeeded. He had his arm around the body. But how to draw it back onto the ledge, while the shirt was transfixed by that branch and the coat was drawn up over the boy's head?

He lay there, with his arm around Harold Sims, wondering what to do next. He knew the boy was alive. He held him so firmly that he could feel the heart beat, the blood pulsing. All the more care, then. He must risk nothing. He tried to ease the weight inward, toward the ledge, but the branch through the shirt groaned. Or was it Sims returning to consciousness?

"Margaret! Any sign of them? I can't hold on much longer, and I can't move him."

It was not Margaret who answered.

"Here we are, Tom!" cried Billy. "Your father's here and Peter Apps. We've got the ropes."

Tom's reaction was extraordinary. "They're swimming out to sea," he gasped, still holding firmly to the body.

"I know, but Father is down there. He heard the dog and was out to see what was happening. He went down to the gully."

Tom went blind for a moment. The strain on his arms was becoming unbearable. He opened his eyes to see a fishing boat rounding from the estuary. It was closing around on the doe and her fawn. All was like dream play in the gathering twilight.

"There they are, Tom!" It was his father's voice. "Give no heed to that. They'll be safe enough. Now here comes the rope. Can't you pull him in?"

"No, he's fixed by this branch. If I pull, it may break before I can get a firm hold."

182

"Look, boy. I've made a loop. Try and get it around him, and we'll tighten up from here, to carry the weight. Then you'll have to cut that bough away."

"Where's Margaret?" cried Tom, suddenly bereft of confidence.

"She's gone to fetch more help and a stretcher," cried Billy. "She's plucky enough, Tom."

Tom's father was an expert in the use of ropes. "There's two coming down, Tom. Put one around yourself first, and we'll hold you. Can you toss the other loop over his head, or does the bough stop that?"

"I can't see very well. But it seems clear, though his coat is drawn up over his head. The branch doesn't protrude. I think I can do it, but I shall have to cut the branch before we can move him."

Down came the two ropes, but it was no easy matter adjusting them. Tom hesitated again. Both arms were engaged. He had not changed the suspension of Harold Sims's body. He risked leaving hold of it. Nothing happened. He dared not put pressure on the hawthorn bush, for it might give way. He wriggled, wormlike, backward from the edge. He could now kneel and put the rope around his own waist.

"I've got that," he called. "It's getting dark now."

His voice seemed forlorn in the twilight. Then he saw a lighted lantern being lowered on a third rope. It moved down the cliffside, its little lozenge of gold competing with the last of daylight down the grazed wall of limestone, where Tom had scrabbled.

"That's better, Dad," he said. He hoped he was shouting, to show his courage, but his voice was weak, his breath short.

Now came the need for skill. Tom too had learned

183

how to handle ropes, as his father's assistant in tree-felling. He rose to his feet, firmly set on the ledge, and took up the second rope, to feel the slackness and ease of the loop. He set the lantern down behind him.

"Now, Dad," he cried, with more strength in his throat. "I'm going to try it. But it will have to be left-handed, for the bush is in my way on the right. I'm casting outward."

He took the loop in his left hand, tried the knot again, swung it to and fro several times, then let it go. His breath went out at the same time.

But all was well. The loop fell over the body, helped by the head's being enveloped in the coat. Tom quickly drew the slipknot tight.

"I've got him," he cried. "It's around his middle."

"Send up that rope from the lantern, Tom," cried Arthur Winter. "We're giving you something to cut that bough."

"But be careful to hold him as it comes away, Dad."

"Aye, lad. Trust us up here."

Arthur sent down a small pruning saw. It was part of his pocket furniture, which he always carried when out-of-doors. Tom drew it down and, without detaching it from the rope, quickly sawed through the branch of hawthorn that might well have been transfixing Harold Sims's body.

Skillful work at the cliff top prevented a jolt to the unconscious boy. Instantly he was drawn up a few inches to compensate for the loss of the dangerous support. He swung around a little, and Tom saw him rise in the air, still an enigmatic shape shrouded in the coat. For a second the lamplight from the back of the ledge passed over him; then he was merely a shadowy object being hauled slowly aloft.

Tom was brought up to find quite a crowd at the cliff top. To his amazement, Mrs. Sims put her arms round him and kissed his dirty face. She had turned from her son, now lying on the stretcher and being examined by the doctor, who had come with Mrs. Sims and Margaret.

Tom saw him kneeling by the stretcher, examining the boy. He heard the doctor say, "There's a broken arm and shoulder and concussion, but I don't think it's worse than that. You've done well, Tom Winter."

Margaret stood near, half-hidden by her stepmother. And Billy was by her side—both his friends rather in the background. But Billy knew what to say:

"They've picked up the deer; both of them are safe, Tom."

He was so tired that he staggered a little and drowsily felt an arm around him, into which he must have stumbled. He believed he was half asleep, but he opened his eyes and saw Sir George Lander towering above him, the lamp at his feet throwing up a shadowy light and adding to the effect of a gigantic but protective figure.

Tom heard him speaking and for a moment could not understand, because he was so weary. But some words took shape.

"Well done, my boy," said Sir George. "We've saved both the little creatures, mother and daughter. The fawn is a doe, Tom. It shall be called yours, though it runs free. Why, boy, it *must* be yours, for as far as I can see, it has been a part of you since it was born."